THE CHRONICLES OF VIKTOR VALENTINE

THE CHRONICLES OF VIKTOR VALENTINE

Z BREWER

Quill Tree Books
An Imprint of HarperCollinsPublishers

Quill Tree Books is an imprint of HarperCollins Publishers.

The Chronicles of Viktor Valentine
 For information address HarperCollins Children's Books, a division of HarperCollins Publishers, 195 Broadway, New York, NY 10007.
www.harpercollinschildrens.com

Library of Congress Control Number: 2023944816
ISBN 978-0-06-324572-3

Typography by Joel Tippie
24 25 26 27 28 LBC 5 4 3 2 1
First Edition

For Jordan Brooks, whom I need in my life today,
today . . . and forever, forever

CHAPTER ONE
The Hunt Begins

As the girl turned the page of the book, the sharp edge of the paper sliced into her finger. With a hiss, she put the injured tip in her mouth, tasting blood. She'd only been pretending to read anyway, desperate to drown out the speaking man's judgmental tone, but so far, her efforts weren't deterring him even a little bit. He hadn't noticed she'd cut herself. Or if he did notice, he didn't seem to care.

"This won't be an easy hunt. He's cunning, this one." Seated in his worn leather club chair, the man was dressed in earth tones, which blended in with the color of the chair. All around him were cardboard boxes bearing labels that listed the contents of each box. Furniture was placed in a haphazard fashion around the room in the careless approach that most movers had when it came to delivering someone else's belongings. On his lap was an old wooden box with an ornate hinge holding the lid closed. "It's going to take every skill we possess to take him down. There cannot be any mistakes."

Wetting her lips, the girl let out a grunt and returned her attention to her book, wishing he'd take the hint. How long was he going to hold the past against her? Would anything she'd ever do be good enough for him?

The woman was crouched by a box on the floor beside his chair, rummaging through its contents with so much purpose that it was giving the girl a headache. "How difficult could it be?" the woman said. "We know where he's located. He has no idea who and what we are, and he's completely unaware that we're here."

The man shook his head, tapping his fingers on the lid of the box. "You underestimate him, just as you underestimated the last one."

He was speaking to the woman, but the girl knew his words were meant for her ears. She'd messed up the last hunt. The woman hadn't been perfect either, but in the end, it was 100 percent the girl's fault that the creature had managed to escape. The man had called her "soft" at the time. But what he really meant was "weak."

Scoffing, the woman said, "What did you expect? It was impossible to get that one alone."

"As I've told you many times, you can't simply pounce. You must get close to them before they realize you're a threat, assure their guard is down, and then strike when they least expect it. Otherwise, you invite . . . complications."

He lifted the latch and opened the wooden box, revealing the contents inside. He began taking stock of what was left. "Your impatience is your greatest weakness."

The last word hung in the air, like smoke. Even when it had dissipated, something of it remained. Giving up on her act, the girl closed the book and set it on her lap. He never would have bought that she'd be so intrigued by the study of weapon making anyway. That was *his* craft. She was just a machine tasked with utilizing the items he made.

As he held one small glass bottle up to the light, the girl cleared her throat and said, "He's younger than I thought he'd be."

Satisfied with the bottle's contents, the man responded, "Older than you think. Trust me. I'm not even sure he realizes his true age."

The girl nodded—not in agreement but in understanding. "So just how do you propose we proceed?"

The man ran his hand lovingly over an object inside the box—a wooden stake tipped in silver. A family heirloom. As he did, the hint of a smile danced on his lips. But when he met the girl's eyes at last, all traces of his smile were gone. "You will do so utilizing your wits and speed . . . and with as much bloodshed as necessary."

"So . . . business as usual, then?" The girl flashed him a smile, hoping to lighten the mood. When he responded by ignoring her quip and turning his attention back to the items inside the wooden case, she muttered under her breath, "Yep. Business as usual."

CHAPTER TWO
Life in the Middle of Nowhere

Viktor Valentine spent a lot of his time hanging out in the middle of Nowhere—both figuratively and literally. Not only was Nowhere the name of his hometown, it was also an accurate description for the place. Nowhere was a destination only to the people who lived there. It wasn't even a place on the way to another place, as the two roads leading into town were long, winding, and out of the way. Maybe three thousand people made up Nowhere's population, and everyone who lived here knew everyone else's name and most everything about one another. When Billie Blathers broke into the mayor's car, everyone knew details within a mere twenty-four hours. And when Stacy Flannigan and Ted Johnson shared their first kiss on the playground, everyone knew that, too. Life in Nowhere was predictable, reliable, and incredibly boring, as far as Viktor was concerned.

That is . . . all but for hanging out with his best friend, Damon MacGregor.

Viktor had known Damon since kindergarten, but they'd been absolute ride-or-die best friends since the second grade, when Damon had stood up for him like nobody ever had. Viktor had been on the swing set, facing away from the elementary school building the way he normally did during recess, when Celeste McDowell approached with her cronies in tow. With one hand on her hip, she said, "Get off! I want to swing now."

Viktor had slowed his swinging, mulling over what to do next. On one hand, he'd only just gotten on. On the other, he'd been bullied by Celeste for as long as he could recall. It didn't help that she lived right next door to him and that, due to his parents' job schedules, he had to walk with Celeste and her mom to school every day. It didn't matter that her mom walked with her. Her mom varied between not paying attention and giggling along with Celeste as she hurled insults at Viktor. It occurred to him even then that bullies create bullies.

Viktor brought his swing to a stop, but just as he was standing up, Damon stepped in behind Celeste and put a frog down the back of her shirt. Viktor wasn't sure where Damon had gotten the frog, or if Damon had just been hanging out, holding some random frog for some strange, unknown reason, and saw an opportunity. But it didn't matter. The frog went down her shirt and Celeste screamed, attracting the attention of every teacher on the playground. Damon was dead for sure. Viktor made a mental note to thank his friend in a touching eulogy. Dead or not, Damon managed a wink at Viktor, even as Mrs. Timmons was dragging Damon to the principal's office—a wink that said, "Hey man, I got your back, no matter what. I'm here for all your random frog-down-the-shirt needs. Till the end."

After school that day, Viktor's mom walked both boys home. Viktor wasn't sure what Damon had said to his mom, even to this day, but from that day on, Viktor walked to and from school with Damon.

Damon . . . who was now almost forty-five minutes late meeting him at the town gazebo.

Viktor pulled his phone from his back pocket and texted his best friend yet again to ask if he was still coming, and for the third time, he received a response from Damon saying that he'd be there in a second. If Viktor's math was right, he'd been waiting for Damon to show up for about a billion seconds, so his best friend owed him big time. But then . . . Damon was always late. Damon's mom once said that Damon was even late to his own birth. Viktor wasn't sure how that would work, but he also wasn't the least bit surprised.

The park was cast in the brilliant hues of dying light as the world moved into that strange place between day and night. Viktor bided his time admiring the most recent graffiti on the inside of the gazebo. He knew who Tara Hasson was. She was an attractive junior at the high school. But he didn't know until now that you could call her "for a good time." And, while he was pretty sure what that meant, he was certain it wasn't something she wanted advertised. As he colored over the name and phone number with a Sharpie, in the distance, at long last, Viktor spied the ever-familiar blue hair of his best friend as he crossed the park to the gazebo.

Damon had been dyeing his hair every color under the sun since they started fifth grade. He started with Kool-Aid packets but moved his way up to actual dye within a matter of months. The cool thing, though, wasn't even his impressive collection of wild colors—peacock blue, cherry red, and neon green among them. It was the way he'd managed to convince his mom that the entire thing was her idea. Viktor's own mom would never even consider him changing his hair. It was boring old black—which she'd call classic, no doubt—all but for a small swatch of bright white behind his left ear. He had no idea if he had something wrong with the pigments in his hair or what. He just knew that in this friendship, Damon was the one with the cool hair, and he was the one with the old-school mom.

When Damon was close enough to see him, Viktor threw his arms up with an air of impatience. Damon pulled the buds from his ears. "What? So I'm a little late."

"A little late? The first time I texted you, you were a little late. By the third time, it's more like rescheduling."

"Quit your bellyaching. I'm here, aren't I?"

Viktor sighed. "Bro, I could've done a million things in the time it took you to get over here."

"Is one of those things protecting someone's reputation with the aid of a marker and hero-like determination?" Damon raised an eyebrow at the fresh scribbles on the gazebo.

Viktor opened his mouth to argue, but then he thought better of lying to his best friend. "The point is, you're late."

Damon looked at him, tilting his head to the side. "I'm always late. You know that. Maybe you need to adjust your clock to Damon Time."

Viktor rolled his eyes and released a frustrated groan. "Maybe you need to adjust your clock to Everyone Else in the Friggin' World Time."

That familiar, sly smile danced across Damon's lips. "Sorry. No can do. Around here it's Damon Time all the time."

"Whatever, dork." Viktor shook his head in defeat, for this was a battle he knew he would not win. "Well, it's too late to see *Dream Killer*. But we could probably catch *Saturday the 14th* if we hurry over to the theater and skip the snack line."

Damon's eyes went wide, as if his friend's words had grabbed his soul and crushed it. "Skip the—what's wrong with you, man? I'm a little late. I didn't kick your cat. Why punish me?"

Viktor sighed. "Fine. But if we miss the previews, you're buying me a super-extra-mondo-large popcorn bucket."

Damon scoffed. "As if any other size will do."

The walk over to Movie Time Cineplex took almost no time at all, but long enough for Viktor and Damon to get into a heated discussion about which was better: summer vacation or winter break.

"I'm just sayin'. You get gifts over winter break." Damon was walking at a pace that said he wasn't exactly in a hurry to get to the movies.

Viktor wondered if it was the movie that he was reluctant to see, or if maybe Damon had made plans with his other friends and just not said anything. It had always just been the two of them, right up until they entered middle school Then Damon got a new group of friends, and Viktor wasn't a part of that group. It felt weird, sharing his best friend. If Viktor were honest with himself, it was annoying too. And kinda lonely. "Yeah, but summer vacation *is* a gift."

"Y'know . . . you've got a point there. A shame it's almost over."

Viktor sighed. The day after tomorrow they'd begin seventh grade at Nowhere Middle School, where fun went to die. Not that school was terrible. It was just boring and oppressive and bossy and lonely and—come to think of it, it was pretty terrible. But the point was, Viktor was about to be a seventh grader and he'd only just really immersed himself into the glory of summer break. He was still reeling from having spent an entire school year under the watchful eye of Mr. Baxter, sixth-grade social studies dictator. The last thing he was looking forward to was a new set of teachers in a new set of classrooms, with a new locker combination to memorize and the same weird green pizza for lunch, served on the same kind of tray that prisoners ate off. He would never understand why some people referred to their tween and teen years as the best days of their life. There had to be more to look forward to at some point. Something new, but not in a horrible way like school stuff. Something . . . exciting.

Damon looked up at the marquee as they approached, sighing at the limited selections. "You sure you wanna see *Saturday the 14th*?"

Viktor rolled his eyes and pulled out the twenty-dollar bill his dad had given him from his front jeans pocket. "Not much choice given how the movie theater is yet another facet of society that does not run on Damon Time."

Damon sighed. "Horror movies were so much better when they were all rated R. PG-13 is just so pathetic. It doesn't matter if you cut the word off with an explosion. It started with *F.* We all know what he said."

"Well, it's better than watching the R-rated ones once they've been edited for TV. Like anybody in the world has ever said 'Let's get the fork out of here.'"

With almost sage-like wisdom, Damon nodded. "Yeah, there is a distinct, tragic lack of cafeteria-based horror movies."

Once they had their tickets and more snacks than were needed to survive a nuclear winter, the two boys entered theater number three and settled into their favorite seats—not too far up and in the direct center of the row. It wasn't all that unusual for them to have the room to themselves when the feature film was horror, and today was no different.

Viktor took a sip of his slushy before setting it in the cup holder. "Kinda sucks that this is our last summer movie before seventh grade."

Damon shrugged, opting to hold his mountain of snacks in an unsteady pile on his lap. "Yeah, but at least we'll be one step closer to ruling the school in the eighth grade."

"What difference does it make? After eighth grade comes ninth, where we're noobs all over again."

"You're missing the point." Shoving a handful of Milk Duds into his mouth, Damon chewed and spoke, leaving Viktor on his own when it came to translating the garbled mess. "The point is that we get to be in charge—if only for a little while."

Viktor rolled his eyes. "Bro, you are grossly overestimating the amount of power a middle schooler is allowed to have. Now please, I'm begging you, don't talk with your mouth full."

Damon grinned and shook his head in defiance, revealing a mouth full of half-chewed caramel and chocolate.

One hour and thirteen bodies (if he was counting right)

into the film, Viktor was berating the actor on-screen for running up the stairs to hide instead of running out of the cabin to look for help, and Damon was chucking kernels of popcorn toward the front of the room in full support of his best friend's critique.

After the credits rolled (thirty minutes and four more bodies later), Viktor shook his head. "That was such a stupid movie."

"I know," said Damon, cracking a grin. "I loved it too."

Once they'd deposited their mountain of trash into the receptacle, Viktor said, "So, what do you wanna do now?"

"Pack my bags and leave Nowhere forever." Damon sighed as they exited the theater and walked out into the night that had fallen while they were watching an innocent camp counselor get their brains bashed in by a teddy-bear monster named Teddy. Viktor still couldn't figure out why the monster had been wearing a mail carrier's uniform, or why his preferred murder weapon was an oversize mallet. But he fought hard not to pick apart the movie plot too much. He knew it hadn't made any sense for a teddy-bear mailman to be so irate and violent with a group of teenage camp counselors, but he'd come for the gore, and the director had delivered on that, at least.

"So, you wanna hang out at my place? I think I figured out where my dad's been hiding his secret chocolate stash."

"Can't," Damon said. "It sucks, but my mom said to get home right after the movie."

Viktor frowned. "That does suck. It's our last weekend before school starts, man."

"Yeah, but it could be worse. I could be stuck in this town till I'm eighteen." Damon threw his arms up in a wave of dramatic sarcasm. "Oh wait! I am!"

Leaving Nowhere was a dream Damon had had since the day he'd turned twelve, just eight months ago. Viktor wondered if it had anything to do with Damon's mom's boyfriend moving into their house, but decided not to ask. If Damon wanted him to know, he'd tell him. Still . . . he did wonder.

"That also sucks. But at least you've got me." Viktor shrugged. It wasn't the best consolation prize, he mused, but it was something.

"You know it, man." Damon held up his fist for a fist bump. "See ya tomorrow? I was thinking we could hang out down at the creek or something. Get some fresh air and some vitamin D."

Viktor raised an eyebrow at the alien that had apparently invaded his best friend's body. Not only was tomorrow the end of their weekend . . . it was also the very last day of summer vacation. There was no way his best friend was suggesting they waste the entire day out in nature, he thought with a shudder. "Is 'something' code for 'ditch all things green and involving bugs and stay indoors playing video games all day and avoiding the sun'?"

Damon held out his hands like they were claws and hissed

up at the sky. "Naturally. But I have to at least tell my mom that I suggested an outdoor option."

A relieved sigh escaped Viktor's lungs. "I was hoping you'd say that. You know how I feel about nature and bugs and stuff. Especially mosquitoes. There are no redeeming qualities in a creature that exists solely on human blood."

As they approached the gazebo, Damon stepped off to the left and started heading home, but not before calling over his shoulder, "Tomorrow, man. You, me, and about a zillion high-definition vampires in 4K resolution. And this time, you better bring your A game."

The corner of Viktor's mouth lifted in a small, reassured smile. "As if I'd bring anything else."

Navigating his way home, Viktor kept to the sidewalks, which were lit by tall, black streetlamps almost the whole way to his house. He counted his steps for a while to occupy his brain, but it wasn't helping all that much. Nighttime made him nervous. It wasn't that he was afraid of the dark. He was just super uncomfortable whenever he thought of what might be lurking *inside* the dark. Even though he knew monsters weren't real, there was this nagging voice at the back of his mind that wondered . . . what if they *were*, though? After all, his imagination was so active that he'd once convinced himself that he was being chased by a shark in a freshwater lake. So, monsters weren't that far out of the realm of possibility. Shaking the thought from his mind—well . . . mostly, anyway—he turned the corner and there, just beyond a block-long pool of darkness, was the house he'd called home since the moment he was born.

It was one of the oldest houses in Nowhere, and it stood out on their block because of it. In fact, it was one of a handful of houses on this end of town that had survived the mass tear-down-and-rebuild efforts of a development company ten years earlier. Their neighbors lived in newer, standard-issue suburban homes—all two-story rectangles in various shades of gray and beige. But Viktor's house stood out. It was purple, for one, with a black slate roof and dark gray trim. The porch was painted gray as well, and the peak above where one would step onto the porch was home to an ornate mosaic featuring a spiderweb of various shapes. At its center was a spider made of black jade—something his mom had explained was intended for protection, but Viktor just called him Harry. Harry Spider.

Because he was funny like that.

Rumor had it their house was built by the town founder, Travion Jett. From what Viktor had come to understand, he was a total weirdo. But he had cool taste in houses, so what did it matter what people said about him?

Viktor took a deep breath and pushed forward into the darkness. When he reached his house and stepped onto the front porch, he let out a sigh of relief, glanced up, and said, "Hey, Harry."

Casting one last look behind him just to be sure that nothing had, in fact, followed him home, Viktor noticed that the lights were on in the empty house across the street. A car was parked in the driveway, which meant that it must not be as empty as it had been for months now. He wondered what his new neighbors would be like, but before he could give it much thought, his front door swung open fast, and his dad moved outside and down the steps faster than it took for Viktor to take in a breath. "Dad? Everything okay?"

His dad came to a stop and turned to face him with a smile. "Everything's fine. I just . . . need to go for a walk."

Viktor could see the tension around that smile. Something was wrong.

Viktor furrowed his brow. "But it's dark out."

There was a long pause where it seemed like his dad was trying to come up with some logical response, but he came up empty. "Keep Hannah and your mom company for a bit, okay? I'll be back."

Not *I'll be back soon*, but *I'll be back*. As if he were reassuring Viktor that this wasn't their final goodbye. Viktor rolled his eyes a little. Parents could be so weird.

As he watched his dad's quick steps carry him down the street, Viktor caught some movement in the corner of his eye. When he turned, he noticed a figure standing in the upstairs window of their new neighbor's house. He couldn't tell if it was a man or woman, an adult or a kid. He just knew that someone was looking at him, and he was looking back. Then without warning, the person's sihouette disappeared.

Curiosity drove him to watch the window. Above him the stars were twinkling their hellos. All around him were the soft sounds of night in suburbia: a cat yowling in the distance, the steady hum of chirping crickets and singing frogs, a far-off car alarm's screams being ignored. It was a pretty normal night in Nowhere, which made it all the more unusual that the tiny hairs on the back of Viktor's neck were standing on end.

"Not just a loser, but a creeper, too, I see," said a nasally voice from the left.

With a sigh, Viktor turned his head to where Celeste was sitting on the swing on her front porch next door. "Hello, Celeste."

Her nose was wrinkled up like he smelled bad or something. He could swear she'd been wearing the same expression ever since the day they met, way back before they even started kindergarten.

Rolling her eyes, she said, "Stop staring at me, creeper-loser, before I tell my dad you're stalking me too."

"Whatever," he mumbled, shaking his head. Viktor turned and opened his front door. The string of bells, crystals, and beads hanging from the door—a gift from his aunt Laura—jingled its welcome. As he stepped over the threshold, the voice at the back of his mind wondered if Dad would be safe out there, with whatever might be lurking in the darkness with him. *Shut up, stupid voice*, he thought as he closed the door behind him. *Dad's tougher than anything he might meet in the dark . . . not that there's anything in the dark.*

Swallowing a worried lump in his throat, he whispered aloud to himself and to the stupid voice in the back of his mind. "Like Mom always says, I'm worrying over nothing again."

CHAPTER THREE
A Question of . . . Well . . . Questions

"Hey, Mom?" Viktor called out, shaking off his still-lingering anxiety.

An assortment of multicolored crystals dripped from the chandelier above, casting tiny rainbows on the tile floor and dark wood walls of the foyer, illuminating the small space in welcoming, warm tones. A fresh arrangement of flowers had been placed on the table to the right of the umbrella stand, and when Viktor inhaled, he could detect the distinct smells of roses, lavender, and eucalyptus.

"In the kitchen, Boog!" Mom's tone wasn't singsongy like usual, which gave him pause, but he brushed it away and joined her.

Their kitchen was larger than most—larger than Damon's, for sure. A barnwood table sat at the center of the room.

At one end was the usual kitchen fare—refrigerator, microwave, stove, cabinets, counters. But at the other end was a fireplace big enough to hold a small cooking cauldron. Mom often hung herbs from the mantel to dry, but every winter, Dad would use the cauldron to cook up the most delicious chili that Viktor had ever tasted.

Viktor plopped down in a dining chair and watched his mom roll out a piecrust on the flour-covered table. "Can you please stop calling me Boog? That was my nickname in the third grade, for cryin' out loud."

His mom furrowed her brow in confusion. "It's still your nickname. But if you don't want me to call you Boog, I'll stop."

Viktor groaned. She'd said that a million times before, but she still kept doing it. It was like parent amnesia or something. "Do you have any idea where Dad's going?"

"Hmm?" It seemed to take some effort for her to tear her attention away from her task. She blinked at him for a second before answering. "Oh. Yes. He's going out for a moonlit stroll. Has a lot on his mind from work, you know."

Viktor was about to ask what sort of things could trouble a custom coffin designer, when Hannah, his eight-year-old sister and biggest pain in his butt, bounded into the room and headed straight for the cookie jar on the counter. But not before sticking her tongue out at her big brother. "Hey, nerd!"

Viktor returned the favor and said, "Hey, brat."

Mom shook her head. "I can never tell if you two are

being mean or endearing to one another."

"Can't it be both?" Viktor chuckled, and then watched his mom return to working the dough. She didn't seem focused on her task so much as she was on something else—maybe whatever it was that had taken Dad out of the house in such a rush. His parents didn't fight very often, and his mom didn't appear upset, so Viktor was pretty sure it wasn't that. But he wasn't convinced it was just work stress that had put that look on his dad's face. "What are you doing, Mom?"

Hannah took a bite of one of the cookies in her hand and said, "Stress baking."

"I'm not stress baking. Everything's fine." Mom picked up the piecrust and placed it in the pie pan she had greased.

Viktor looked at Hannah, who pointed to the two used cookie sheets that were sitting on the stove. She mouthed, "Stress baking."

"Viktor, I saved you a plate of dinner with the silly assumption that you and Damon didn't fill up on junk food at the movies." Glancing at him, she sighed. "But by the look on your face I'm assuming I should be wrapping that up for your lunch tomorrow. Speaking of lunch, are you getting hot lunch on Monday or taking lunch from home?"

Snatching the unbitten cookie from Hannah's hand, Viktor said, "Please don't remind me that Monday is a thing that exists. I am not ready to be a seventh grader."

Mom said, "Oh, I'm sure seventh grade won't be that bad. One year closer to ruling the school."

Was there some pamphlet on school hierarchy being passed around that he wasn't aware of? "Anyway . . . I'll just take some leftover pizza. If there is any."

Mom slid a bowl of fresh strawberries closer to herself and kept chatting as she removed the stems. Apparently, today's stress-baking bonus was a strawberry pie. "I'm assuming this means you and Damon are taking over the living room TV tomorrow to play video games all day and avoid any semblance of fresh air? One last blood-soaked, junk-food-stuffed hurrah before school begins?"

Viktor gave a slight shrug. "Something like that, yeah."

He popped the rest of the cookie into his mouth and chewed, sorry for Mom's stress but thankful for her baking.

"Listen, Viktor." Her hands slowed as she spoke, which meant that whatever she was about to say, it was going to be upsetting for Viktor to hear. Parents like to think they're sneaky, but they have the worst poker faces in the world. "Do you recall Susan, that friend of mine who runs the community vegetable garden?"

"The one with the hippie skirts and all the tattoos?" Licking a bit of melted chocolate from the corner of his mouth, he opened the lid of the cookie jar and took three cookies out, sitting one of them in front of Hannah. "What about her?"

"Well, her cousin just accepted a position at the middle school as the new librarian and—"

"What happened to Mrs. Driscoll?" Mrs. Driscoll was

the meanest adult that Viktor had ever had the displeasure of knowing. She'd once given him detention for breathing too loudly in the library. And that was her on a nice day. "Y'know what? Forget it. Good for hippie Susan's cousin."

"Right? She's just so excited. It's a wonderful opportunity for her." Her voice trailed off in a way that drew Viktor's eyebrows together in suspicion.

"But?"

"There's no *but*."

"There's always a *but*." He took a big bite of one of the cookies, but it was hard to focus on the yummy chocolate in his mouth when there was clearly a *but* lurking somewhere in this conversation.

Hannah giggled and stole a strawberry from the bowl. "Only when you're in the room, ya butt."

Viktor plucked a discarded stem and tossed it at his sister, tagging her on the nose.

Mom continued as if nothing were happening between the siblings. "Taking over this position as middle school librarian is a big deal and can be challenging for anyone—especially someone who's new to town."

Pointing the last half of his cookie at his mom, he said, "I still feel like there's a *but*, Mom."

"You won't miss out on any important classes and won't have to stay after school to help, as it's during a free period. Get her through this first school year with a friendly face. I already discussed it with your counselor and principal and everyone's on board with it."

"Wait, what?" He swallowed the bite of cookie in his mouth, but it took its time going down. "You volunteered me to help out the new librarian without even asking me?"

"What's wrong? It's not like it'll interfere with your after-school plans."

"What about my in-school plans?" he muttered.

As if he had any in-school plans other than survive, he thought with an internal eye roll.

"If you were new to a school, I'm sure you'd appreciate a little assistance while you adapted to your surroundings." She met his eyes with that no-nonsense look all moms had. "And being that I have raised two loving, generous, kind souls, I assume this won't be a problem."

Viktor groaned. "And I'd be a real jerk by saying no now, huh?"

Mom rummaged through a drawer for a paring knife and began slicing the berries. "I promise that next time I'll ask well in advance, but I would appreciate it if you'd do this for me. Besides . . . you could use a little more time in the library. Might help you pass English this year." When she looked at him again, he could almost hear his freedom shrinking.

"Is there any chance at all that you're joking?"

Mom met his eyes, and he could see that the answer was a hard no. "It's just for the school year. It'll give you something productive to do. And before you even say it—no, playing video games with Damon isn't productive."

She was wrong, of course, but she wasn't so different from many people. Too many parents were under the impression that video games were bad for you, but Viktor had read somewhere that playing video games improved hand-eye coordination and deductive reasoning skills, with the added bonus of the joy of blowing fictional people or monsters to smithereens.

Under his breath, Viktor said, "You've never tried to get past level thirteen of *All the Vampires Everywhere.*"

Mom said, "What was that?"

"Nothing." Viktor felt a bit like he was sinking. It was one thing to volunteer for something. It was quite another to be volun-told. "I'm gonna hang out in my room for a while."

Mom said, "Don't forget to put your laundry in the chute."

"Yeah, don't forget your laundry, ya butt." Hannah giggled and stuck out her tongue again, to which Viktor responded in kind. The truth was, he adored his little sister. Even when she was being a butt.

As he made his way upstairs, his mood soured. It was bad enough that so many of the kids he knew were spending their summers traveling to amazing places and he was stuck in Nowhere. But now he was expected to spend his entire seventh-grade year hanging out in a quiet room with a zillion dusty books and zero video games or fun? It wasn't fair. His mom could've at least asked him.

He opened his door and gathered the armload of laundry

that had been covering his bedroom floor for days. After a quick trip down the hall, he dumped all of it down the laundry chute, then paused to jab at the clothing with a broom handle. Then, with heavy steps, he went back to his room, slipped inside, and closed the door.

Viktor's bedroom was on the smaller side but made up for the lack of space with cool, angular walls that gave it more of a hexagon shape than a traditional square. On the wall above his bed hung his prized possession—an autographed poster of his favorite band, the Screaming Meemies. His bedroom was the only room in the house with a balcony. It wasn't a large space—just big enough to hold two old dining chairs and a small table—but it was his sacred place where he went when he needed time to think. Or pout, which he was only doing a little of now and wouldn't admit to even under intense torture, which it sounded like volunteering at the library was totally going to be.

The night air was warm and welcoming when he stepped outside. He saw two bats flying overhead, clearing the sky of pesky bugs, pollinating flowers, dispersing the seeds of hundreds of species of plants, and just generally making the world a better place to live in. He'd always wondered how some people could not like bats. They were ecological heroes! Plus, they had sweet little smooshed-up faces and leathery wings. Viktor, for one, was a big fan, and he didn't care who knew it or disagreed with his views. Science, as it always was, was on his side.

The sky was filled with stars—inky black with diamond accessories. That was one good thing about Nowhere—even though it was a town, it wasn't so big that the streetlights made it difficult to see the stars at night. Viktor was grateful for that. The stars, after all, made him feel a little less lonely on lonely-feeling nights.

He'd hoped Damon was going to be able to hang out some more after the movie, but moms were moms, and their instructions might as well have been carved in stone. Like, for instance, if a mom volunteered you for something, you were going to do that something, whether you liked it or not. Not that Viktor had anything against the library. It just wasn't where he wanted to spend the entire school year.

The sound of lilting giggles drew his attention to the street below. A group of five kids around his age was walking down the street toward the park. Viktor couldn't quite make out what they were saying. He recognized two of the kids as Taylor Whitmer and Drew Gysen. Upon further examination, he realized that the two girls were Janie Brooks . . . and Celeste McDowell, who was looking almost like a normal human being—and not a fire-breathing jerk—under the light of the full moon. He sank back into the shadows of his balcony and watched, wishing more than anything that he had people to hang out with at night . . . and that one of those people was anybody but Celeste.

Familiar laughter tore through the night again, and Viktor focused his attention on the third guy in the group. When he recognized who it was—the blue hair didn't lie, after all—his heart shrank and fell to the bottom of his stomach.

Why would Damon lie about having to go home after the movie? His friend had never lied to him before—not that he knew of. Why would he start now? And even if Damon hadn't lied—even if something had changed after he got home, and his mom said it was fine for him to go out again—why hadn't he asked Viktor to come along?

Viktor watched them until they rounded the corner, then he sat and admired the stars for what seemed like an eternity—all the while wondering and worrying.

A strange feeling settled on him, as if he were being watched. He examined the yard, the street, and settled on the window of his new neighbor's house, where someone had been standing earlier. Once more, he saw a figure there, but this time, the person pulled the curtains back and offered him a wave. A girl who Viktor didn't recognize. Even from a distance, he could make out that her hair was deep ruby red, her skin pale. He was willing to bet she had freckles but had no reason for thinking so, apart from his imagination asking him questions that he didn't have any answers to. She was cute. Very cute. So cute, in fact, that his stomach was beginning to feel a bit queasy, but in the best way possible.

At first Viktor was too stunned to breathe, let alone respond. But once he wrapped his head around the fact that he wasn't dying of a heart attack, he raised his hand and waved back.

With a smile, she drew the curtains closed. A moment later the light flicked off.

He was about to retreat into his bedroom, when he noticed his dad hurrying up the street toward their house with a wild look in his eye. *Totally normal behavior there, Dad*, Viktor thought. *Nothing at all to question about that.*

As he stepped back into his room, the voice at the back of his mind began to speak—pointing out that it *was* kind of strange for his dad to leave the house so late, and very strange that he'd come back looking so out of sorts—but he squashed the voice before he could hear it with any kind of clarity.

Lying back on his bed after changing into his pajamas, Viktor closed his eyes and sighed, flirting with sleep. Tomorrow there would be time for questions, but all tonight held time for was rest.

And with any luck, dreams about the cute stranger across the street who'd waved at him.

CHAPTER FOUR
RIP Viktor's Freedom

The next morning, Viktor was woken by the sun, which had forced its way into his room through the small crack between the curtain panels. He rolled out of bed, grumbling, "Stupid morning. Stupid sun with its stupid vitamin D."

The smell of bacon drew him downstairs. If he was going to be forced to be awake this early, he might as well be filling his stomach with handfuls of yumminess.

His dad was sitting in his favorite recliner in the living room, relaxing into its worn leather while he nursed a cup of coffee and read the newspaper, which said something about his dad's age. Who read actual newspapers anymore? Everything anyone ever wanted or needed to know was online. But then, his dad had always had a difficult time with change. As if demonstrating this, the built-in bookcase behind his dad's chair was filled with all sorts of vintage and antique books that no one in the family but Dad ever read.

"Morning, Dad."

From behind his newspaper, Dad said, "Good morning, Viktor. Sleep well?"

"Yeah. I mean, okay, I guess." Viktor looked at the coffee mug. It was his dad's favorite. On one side was the symbol and contact info for their local Red Cross. On the other was a picture of a mosquito and the words "Careful! I bite!" Dad loved that mug. Dad loved a lot of weird things. "I'm gonna go grab something to eat."

"Speaking of breakfast, I have a question for you." Dad lowered the paper and smiled. His dark eyes were sparkling in that telltale obnoxious way that told Viktor he was about to be faced with something groan-worthy, for sure.

Taking a slow, deep breath in preparation, Viktor said, "Oh yeah? What's that?"

"Why don't eggs tell jokes?" His dad's lips were pursed like he was holding back laughter. "They'd crack each other up!"

Rolling his eyes in response, Viktor sighed and walked into the kitchen where Mom was moving crisp bacon from the pan to a plate covered with paper towels. "Mom, can't you talk to him? Get him to stop with the dad jokes?"

Without turning to face him, Mom said, "Which would you rather he stops—the dad jokes or the puns?"

Sitting at the table with a groan, he replied, "Both isn't an option?"

Hannah bounded into the room and took a seat across from him. "I like Dad's jokes. They're funny."

With his attention still on his mom, he said, "This one's gonna be a real problem in a year or two. Then they'll both be telling terrible jokes."

"You'll survive." Mom turned from the stove at last, a small smile on her lips. "Bacon?"

"Thanks." She set the plate on the table, and Viktor grabbed two slices and took a bite of one. As he chewed it, his imagination filled with the notion of all-day video games and junk food with his best friend. At least his summer was ending on a high note.

As Dad entered the kitchen for a coffee refill, Viktor said, "Hey, Dad, did you see we have new neighbors?"

Dad was silent long enough to make Viktor wonder if he'd heard him. He was about to repeat himself when his dad said, "Do we now?"

"Viktor." Mom paused then, as if she were uncertain what she'd meant to say. "Can you take the trash out to the bin and take the bin out to the road please?"

"Can't I do it after I shower? I'd rather not show off my pajama pants to the entire neighborhood."

"What's the matter? Afraid the new neighbor girl will see your cute li'l jammies?" Hannah giggled and continued downing the piece of toast she was holding.

Truth be told, Viktor liked his pajamas. They were comfy and soft, with just the right amount of bagginess. So who cared that they were covered in little red smiley faces? "Shut up. I just don't wanna be seen in public wearing my pajamas."

Mom and Dad were carrying on a silent conversation with their eyes. Viktor had seen it countless times before. He just wasn't sure why.

At last, Mom said, "Of course, honey. You can wait until you're dressed. But do that now, please. Before you forget."

Viktor shoveled the last half of a strip of bacon into his mouth, then slouched his way back upstairs. His feet felt like somebody had replaced them with blocks of concrete. What did parents have against easing into your day, anyway?

He grabbed some clothes from his dresser and headed into the bathroom. As he stood under the hot water, he kicked himself for acting like such a baby. For the second day in a row, he was pouting over something that was out of his control. It must be nice to be in charge, and it was clear that Mom knew she was and everybody in his family knew it too. Heck, Dad even called her "my darling countess" when he was being all gross and mushy with her. So what choice did Viktor have but to put on some stupid pants and take out the stupid garbage?

None, he thought. *Not even a stupid little bit.*

Once his teeth were brushed, his hair dried, and his definitely-not-pajamas clothes were on, he headed back downstairs. He wasn't surprised that no one was at home at that point. Dad had to take Hannah to her friend's house on his way to work and Mom had some big meeting down at the blood drive. They were a busy family, even on a Sunday, and it wasn't a big deal to find himself on his own.

While slipping his shoes on, Viktor did what he could to accept that summer was really, truly over before grabbing the garbage from the kitchen and stepping out the front door. As he tossed the bag into the trash bin, he heard a familiar voice chime, "Hey, man. What's up?"

Normally, he was happy to hear his best friend's voice, but this time, Viktor couldn't help but feel a little annoyed. How could Damon just ditch him for his group of friends like he did last night? Not to mention that he chose to hang out with Celeste.

"Forced labor," Viktor said as he turned to face Damon.

Damon brushed his blue hair from his eyes and raised an eyebrow. "Uh-oh. What is it this time? Mowing the lawn? Cleaning your room?"

"Trash duty. And it gets worse." Viktor sighed. "Starting tomorrow, I have volunteer work. At the library. All school year."

"Oof." Damon shook his head in horror. "Brutal."

"Yeah . . ." As he gripped the handle of the trash bin and wheeled it to the street, he looked up at the window where he'd seen the girl the night before. There was no sign of her now.

"So . . . does that mean no vampire killing today? Or . . . ?"

Viktor counted his breaths for a heartbeat, the image of Damon laughing along with his new friends as they passed by Viktor's house dancing in his mind's eye, knowing that Viktor had a balcony . . . and that he was out there almost every night. "If that were the case, I'm sure you'd find someone else to hang out with."

"Huh?" He could feel Damon's eyes on him as Damon said, "What's that supposed to mean?"

"You could've just told me you had plans to be with your friends last night, Damon. You didn't have to lie to protect my feelings or whatever."

"Bro, what are you talking about?"

"I was on my balcony and saw you with Taylor, Drew, Janie, and . . . Celeste." Swallowing the growing lump in his throat, Viktor followed it up with, "Not that I care, but still."

Good save, Viktor. Nice and smooth.

Damon grabbed his shoulder and gave it a squeeze. "Listen . . . after I got home, my mom gave me a list and sent me to the store for some stuff. I was headed there when I ran into those guys, so we walked together for a while. Celeste kinda jumped in with us at the last minute."

Viktor wanted to believe him. In fact, he had no reason not to. But sometimes he wondered why someone awesome and funny and cool like Damon would want to hang out with the likes of him. The truth was, Damon was his only real friend.

"I wouldn't lie to you, Viktor. I may be a lot of things, but a liar isn't one of them." Damon held his gaze, driving his point home.

Viktor shrugged, swallowing again to try to prevent a new lump from forming in his throat. He hated that he was so insecure sometimes. "It's okay if you have other friends, Damon. I get it."

"I do have other friends." It was Damon's turn to shrug. "But none of them are my *best* friend. That job's taken by you till the end of time, remember?"

It was hard to remember, but Viktor knew it to be true, and no one and nothing could ever come between them. He was almost positive. Not far behind that thought was the memory of the girl in the window. "Hey, new subject, did you see someone moved into that empty house across the street from mine?"

"I saw the lights were on last night, yeah. Have you met the new neighbors yet?"

"Not yet. But I saw a girl looking out her window at me." He bit his bottom lip. "I mean, I think she was looking at me. She probably wasn't."

"Dude. You don't know that. She might've been leaning up against the window, fogging up the glass with her breath while a small trail of drool dripped down her chin just at the sight of you." Damon offered him a grin and a knowing look. "You don't know how girls are."

"Neither do you."

Damon paused, considering this for a moment before responding. "You may have a point, but still. Don't count yourself out like that. I'm sure there's a girl out there somewhere that finds your particular type of charm irresistible."

From two houses down, Viktor's now-retired fifth-grade teacher, Mrs. Caddleston, smiled her denture-filled smile and offered them a wave. "Good morning, boys."

"Told ya so. And just look at that walker." Damon waggled his eyebrows, soliciting a light punch in the arm from Viktor, who was both rolling his eyes and stifling a laugh at the same time.

Viktor waved to be nice, but muttered to Damon, "Bro, shut up."

When Mrs. Caddleston had turned back toward her house, Damon's tone shifted from obnoxious to his usual nonchalance. "So are we killing vampires all day or not?"

Viktor allowed a smile to settle on his lips. For the moment, there was no school, no library, no Celeste, and no questioning his best friend's loyalty. "As if there's any better way to spend our last day of freedom. You grab the chips. I'll grab the controllers."

The front door opened later that afternoon and Viktor's dad stepped inside, his briefcase in one hand and a cup of boba tea in the other. Whatever flavor it was, it looked dark red, with what seemed to be grape bursting boba at the bottom. Viktor raised an eyebrow. "Since when do you drink boba tea, Dad?"

"Since I found a place that makes it right," he replied, dropping his briefcase beside his recliner and nodding toward the TV. "What are you boys playing?"

Damon said, "*All the Vampires Everywhere.* Your character's a Slayer who must clear an entire town of a horde of bloodthirsty vampires before their king arrives."

"Hmm. Interesting. And who's their king?"

Viktor shrugged. "I think it's supposed to be Dracula, but they never say."

The corner of Dad's mouth lifted in an appreciative smile. "Sounds like a formidable foe."

"I wouldn't know." Viktor groaned as the monsters on-screen swarmed over his and Damon's avatars, leaving nothing but red streaks behind. "Can't make it past this stupid level."

"Well, when you manage to encounter Dracula . . ." As he left the room, he raised his boba tea in a toast to the two boys before taking a sip. ". . . let me know."

Damon shook his head as he reached into the Doritos bag for some of the remaining crumbs. "Your dad is so weird sometimes."

Viktor rolled his eyes. "Sometimes? He's weird all the time."

Picking up his controller again, Damon brushed the crumbs from his shirt and said, "Dude, help me clear this room and we can tackle that big guy together."

Viktor groaned. "What's the point? He squashes my head

like an overripe grape every time!"

"Did you try weakening him with garlic?"

Damon said it like it was the most obvious thing in the world, but if that were true, they would have finished this level ages ago. Still, without a word, Viktor hit the button that made his avatar spray down the monster with a healthy dose of garlic juice. The vampire fell to the ground, moaning. Viktor hit Turbo and beheaded the beast, then sat back, staring at the corpse on the screen in wonder. "Huh. Garlic. Who knew?"

The corner of Damon's mouth lifted in a knowing smirk. "I suspect the Italians."

CHAPTER FIVE
Welcome to the Dungeon

Before Viktor even opened his eyes that Monday morning, he knew it was going to be the longest day of his entire life.

With a groan reserved for such an occasion, he sat up in bed and rubbed the sleep from his eyes with one hand while stabbing at his phone screen to turn off his alarm with the other. As he stretched, he heard Hannah singing along (*almost* on key) to the latest hit song in the bathroom next door.

"Viktor, are you up?" Mom called from downstairs.

"Yes!" He yawned, stretching his arms way above his head for a moment. "Unfortunately."

"You'd better get in the shower, or you'll have no time for breakf—"

"I know!" He knocked hard on the bathroom door, but it wasn't like he did it to be obnoxious. Any softer and his sister wouldn't have heard him over her pop celebration of feminism. "C'mon, Hannah, it's my turn. Continue your concert somewhere else."

"Sorry, can't hear you over the sound of my awesome!"

"Hannah, come on!"

The music turned off and Hannah cracked open the door. "Like you're in any kinda hurry to go to school. Didn't you barely pass English last year?"

Viktor narrowed his eyes and leaned closer. He kept his voice steady and calm as he said, "Go elsewhere."

"I planned on it." She sashayed past him and made her way downstairs with a bounce in her step that Viktor would never understand.

By the time he finished his shower and got dressed, he was again the only person left in the house. Just the muted ghost smells of bacon greeted him in the kitchen, along with a sticky note on the fridge that read "Waffles in the freezer!"

Sighing, he grabbed the yellow box and settled in for a toaster breakfast on what should have been a bacon-and-eggs kind of day. As he pressed the lever down on the toaster, his phone buzzed to life.

Damon: Hey dude. You ready for this?

Viktor: Does it matter? Like death and taxes, man, the seventh grade is unavoidable.

Damon: Somebody's feeling chipper this morning. Be there in ten.

After he'd eaten and put his plate and fork in the dishwasher, Viktor slung his messenger bag over his shoulder and headed out the front door, making certain to lock it behind him. As he slid his house key into his front jeans pocket, a flash of blue just to the left caught his attention.

"Hey man." Damon's hair was looking particularly cool this morning—spiked up in a way that resembled a Mohawk but wasn't one.

Viktor sighed. "Hey."

"You okay?"

"I'm fine. Just dreading the idea of another school year full of homework and the constant fear of detention."

Damon chuckled and shook his head. "Your optimism, bro. It's my favorite thing about you." With a grin, he gave Viktor a playful smack on the back. "Come on, let's go."

It wasn't a long walk to the school, but it was long enough for reality to hit Viktor hard. He was a seventh grader. There was no going back now.

Minutes later, the boys arrived at the building that sat at the town's center, ready to begin their nine-month-long sentence of the seventh grade. Nowhere Middle School was about as plain and ordinary as any other middle school on the planet. Except for one undeniably weird thing: the bronze statue of their mascot that stood just outside the front doors, waiting to greet students and staff. Upon first glance, or if you only saw it from the back, it looked like what most people would consider to be a statue of an ordinary man. But from the front, it looked like some kind of deranged butler holding out a platter in front of him, upon which was an assortment of oddities. A Barbie-size bigfoot, Mothman, the Jersey Devil, and so many more. Tying it all together was the large engraving at the base of the statue, which read "Welcome to Nowhere Middle School: Home of the Cryptids!"

What made matters worse is that no one knew who the butler guy was or why he was serving up creatures that didn't exist on a platter. Apparently, Viktor wasn't alone in finding the whole thing difficult to wrap his head around, though, because rather than translate the monstrosity of the mascot statue into a costume to be worn during sports games, the PTA had opted to spring for a costume of what looked like a green, spiky goblin with big red eyes that lit up. Rumor had it, it was supposed to be a chupacabra.

Viktor thought it looked more like the stuff of nightmares.

Damon smacked him on the back and said, "Mark my words, my friend. Seventh grade is just going to be a preview for when we rule the school next year."

Truth be told, Viktor didn't really care about ruling the school. He was more worried about surviving it unscathed.

Outside the front doors were four tables, each labeled with a portion of the alphabet so students could pick up their schedule by last name. The line at Damon's table was the longest, but as usual, there weren't a lot of people waiting at the "U-to-Z" table. As Viktor approached, the woman sitting behind the table smiled. "Viktor Valentine!"

"Hi, Ms. Carnes."

"I believe I have you in my art class this year. It's gonna be fun."

"Yeah. I mean . . ." As he took the paper from her, his brain scrambled, and he 100 percent forgot how to act like a normal human being. "Yeah. Uhh . . . sorry."

Her smile never faltered. "Have a great first day, Viktor."

"Thanks," he mumbled as Damon rejoined him in front of the doors, gripping his own schedule in his hand. "So, what's the damage?"

Viktor scanned the piece of paper. "English first thing in the morning, which is bad enough. But it looks like I've got Mrs. Harkins."

Damon shook his head in a show of empathy. "Yeah, that's not ideal, for sure. Harkins is a billion years old and hates everyone. I heard she assigns homework every night. I also heard she kinda looks like a toad."

"Great. Just . . . great." After emitting a helpless sigh, Viktor ran down the list in his hand. "Then I've got math, PE, lunch, library assistance, social studies, art, and science."

"Sweet. It looks like we've got PE, lunch, and science together, so all hope of getting through this year relatively sane isn't quite lost yet. What's your locker number?"

"It's 131."

"Bro." A grin spread across Damon's face. "I'm 132. Noice!"

The bell rang and all the students and staff who were still outside rushed indoors in an almost fluid motion. With a sigh, he looked at Damon. "Well . . . see ya, man."

"Don't do anything I wouldn't do."

Viktor walked in and was immediately caught up in a sea of students until he found his way to room 31, where he'd been sentenced to hours of English for the next nine months of his life.

"Take a seat, everybody. Wherever you want." Viktor suppressed a groan. Teachers loved saying that students could sit anywhere they'd like. It made them seem kind and approachable. But everybody knew that after a few weeks of offering freedom, the teacher would have identified the troublemakers and assigned seating would become a thing. It never failed.

Of course, a quick glance at the speaker told him that she wasn't the teacher anyway. She looked far too young and far too cool to be an ancient, toad-like homework overassigner. Her hair lay on her shoulders in waves of dark purple that Viktor thought were black until the light caught it. She had a tasteful nose ring, and her eyes were lined in thick black kohl. She might have been a student teacher, here to assist, but there was no way she was teaching. Teachers couldn't look that cool. It was in the handbook or something.

Viktor chose a seat closest to the door. That way he could be the first to escape once the bell had rung at the end of class. He didn't feel that way about all his classes, but English had never been his thing. Reading in general, for that matter. There were a million other things that he could entertain himself with that weren't sitting and staring at words on a page.

"Welcome! If you're looking for Mrs. Harkins's English class, you're in the right place. Mrs. Harkins fell ill, so until she gets back, I'll be your substitute teacher. You can call me Mrs. McMillan, but most people just refer to me by my first name, October." The substitute smiled and shuffled through some papers on the desk. Her nails had been painted to match her hair, but with tiny moons and stars in silver and white. "Now, Mrs. Harkins left a lot of detailed notes on what we should be doing every day until she gets back. . . ."

The corners of October's painted burgundy lips tugged down, as if she wasn't at all impressed by the instructions that Mrs. Harkins had provided.

"But, to be honest, it looks like a lesson plan from twenty years ago, and that's no fun, so if you guys are cool with it, I'm gonna shake things up a little. But before we get started, let's begin with some introductions." She picked up a list from the top of her desk and scanned the names on it. With a last name like Valentine, Viktor was way down in the alphabet, so it would be a minute before she called on him—something Viktor considered to be no small blessing. "Let's start with the end of the alphabet, shall we?"

Oh no. His heart launched into a mini panic attack.

"Viktor Valentine?" She swept her eyes over the students

and settled on Viktor, who was trying in desperation not to bolt for fear of public speaking. "Why don't you stand up and tell us something about yourself. Anything that you'd like to share."

It didn't take an hour for Viktor to stand up beside his desk, but it felt like it. His throat felt like sandpaper, and he tried clearing it, but it didn't help. What also didn't help was the fact that one teacher and nineteen other seventh graders were staring at him, waiting for him to say something.

"I . . . uhh . . . my name's Viktor . . . ?" Mortified at the sound of his own voice, Viktor coughed into his fist. "I guess you could say I'm pretty obsessed with this band called the Screaming Meemies. They're a little Concrete Blonde, mixed with a healthy dose of the Pixies and a dash of My Chemical Romance."

Relief flooded through him as he sank back in his seat, ready for the sub to move on to the next name on the list. But then, from somewhere in the back of the class, someone muttered, "Loser."

The laughter that followed made it so much worse.

He didn't look for whoever had said it. It didn't matter. What did matter was that October's eyes snapped right to a kid in the back of the class and said, "That's the last time that happens in this classroom. Got it? We should be lifting one another up, not shoving one another down. Let's remember that, okay?"

No one responded, but the air in the room had changed.

October wasn't the type of sub to take crap from anyone. Viktor liked that.

"You have great taste, Viktor. That's my favorite band too." He doubted it, because what adult actually knew about the Screaming Meemies? But it was a nice thing to say. After flashing him a kind smile, she glanced down at the list she was holding. "Let's see . . . Emma Thomas?"

One by one, each student shared with the class a little something about themselves. Viktor sank further down in his seat, just waiting for it to be over. After everyone had been equally mortified, October said, "And I know this isn't alphabetical, but my name is October McMillan and I firmly believe that every day is Halloween if you want it to be."

There were some mutterings from the back of the class, but they died down quickly. Something told Viktor his classmates knew better than to mess with this sub. October smiled and held up a book for everyone to see. The cover was red with an image of fangs on the front. "Okay, class. This is *Dracula*. It was first published in 1897, and we're kicking off the school year with a bang."

More like with a fang, Viktor thought with a chuckle that he didn't give voice to.

October glanced his way, the corners of her lips tugging up in a smile that gave Viktor pause. "This book is one of my personal favorites. Over the next week, we're going to read it and, based on what you learn during that reading, you're then going to write a paper describing what a vampire like Dracula would look like in the modern age."

"I have a question." The blond girl in the seat next to Viktor's raised her hand as she spoke. "I don't get it."

October chuckled. "That's not a question, but go ahead. What don't you understand?"

"Like . . . what's this all about? What are we supposed to write?"

October nodded for a moment before answering, as if gathering her thoughts. "Well, it's a speculative piece, so . . . for instance, would vampires live openly in the present, side by side with humans? Or would they be more stealth like Dracula was? How would they eat without giving away their secret? There are all sorts of questions to explore. So, like, get creative. Have fun with it. And if you'd like some more recommendations on vampires in fiction, I'll be happy to oblige. It just so happens to be a favorite subject of mine."

By the time class ended, Viktor was feeling a lot more optimistic about English and seventh grade in general. So when the bell rang, he moved out the door with a surprising bounce in his step.

But that bounce fell flat the moment Viktor saw the group that had formed next to his locker. Taylor Whitmer, Drew Gysen, Janie Brooks, and Celeste McDowell were standing in a semicircle around Damon, who was holding a flyer in his hand advertising some big party and checking out the size of his locker. With a deep breath, Viktor approached and wedged his way behind Drew so he could reach his own locker door. As he fiddled with the combination lock, Damon noticed him and said, "Hey, man. How are you navigating the gauntlet of the seventh-grade experience so far?"

Viktor shrugged. "It's been surprisingly smooth. But then . . . math and PE are next, so the entire day is about to go in the toilet."

"It's pretty much a guarantee that math will be its usual third circle of hell, but PE shouldn't be too bad. First-day gym class oughta be cake. The only question is . . . what flavor? Dodgeball or badminton?"

Celeste and Janie were comparing their first days, while Taylor and Drew started messing around with a Frisbee Taylor had apparently found on the ground outside before the first bell had rung. While they were distracted, Viktor leaned closer to Damon and said, "You wanna hang out after school?"

"No can do, amigo." Damon stuffed the flyer in his hand inside his backpack, shut his locker, and spun the combination lock around to make sure it was locked. "I've already been sentenced. My mom insists that Stepdad-to-be and I bond over undercooked spaghetti tonight."

"Gross."

"It's not so bad if you know what to expect."

"I was talking about the forced socializing with her boyfriend."

"Yeah, so was I." The ring of the bell almost drowned out the sound of Damon's sigh. Almost.

Viktor gave him a gentle slap on the back. "First things first. Let's survive the rest of the school day."

Damon swung his backpack over one shoulder and offered Viktor a nod. "See ya in PE, Valentine."

As expected, math class was as boring as watching paint dry. PE was a celebration of the jocks and the teacher, Mr. Brock, pointing out the weaknesses of everybody else in class. But without fail, lunch was the reprieve for the entire day—the one period where no one expected anything of students but for them to sit and eat, which just so happened to be two of Viktor's favorite activities.

Except . . .

"Oh no." Viktor opened his messenger bag and rifled around but came up empty. The two slices of pizza he'd wrapped up for lunch were sitting on the second shelf of his refrigerator at home. "Crap!"

Damon approached holding a tray covered with enough food to satisfy a zillion armies. "Forget your lunch?"

"Yeah. Hey, do you have two bucks I can borrow? If my mom finds out I forgot my lunch, she may kill me."

"Gotcha covered, man. Can't have you dying over a couple of slices of pepperoni."

For a brief second, a girl's red hair caught Viktor's attention. It wasn't dark and rich, though—not at all like the new neighbor girl. But it did make him pause and think about her for a second.

Damon followed Viktor's gaze. "Looking for someone?"

Viktor shrugged. "That girl I saw in the window the other night? The new neighbor? I kinda thought she'd be here today."

"Maybe she was just visiting family or something. Just 'cause you saw her there doesn't mean she lives there."

"Yeah, maybe." He tried hard to keep the sound of disappointment out of his voice but failed.

Damon slipped his hand into his front jeans pocket and retrieved a five-dollar bill. "Go grab some food, dude. I'll save you a spot."

"Thanks, man. But . . ." Viktor tried to think of a cooler way to ask but came up empty. "Can it just be us? I mean, it's the first day, dude. Can we wait a day before you force me to be social?"

Damon pretended to think it over for several seconds before responding. "Okay, but you owe me one, Valentine."

Once he'd polished off what kind of resembled a burger and fries and the bell had rung once more, Viktor said his goodbyes to his best friend and headed down the hall to the open double doors just opposite the main office. Above the doorway hung a simple sign that read "Library."

The library looked pretty much as it had the last time Viktor had been inside of it, which was last year, just before the school science fair. He'd been building a small robot for his entry, but there was a huge problem with that that he hadn't quite considered—Viktor had no idea at all how to build a robot. Lucky for him, librarians pretty much know everything, and he managed to score a B-minus. Even though the robot set the table on fire. Twice.

After navigating the rows for a bit, he found the new librarian on her knees, organizing one of the lower shelves of the science fiction section. "Hey, Mrs. Conrad. My mom said I—"

"Ah, yes. My first victim." Mrs. Conrad stood, smiled, and rubbed her palms together, sealing Viktor's fate. "Welcome to the dungeon, Viktor Valentine. We've got a lot of work to do."

CHAPTER SIX
Appetites

"So . . ." Viktor flicked a glance around the room, taking in the shelves and shelves of books, as well as the large desk at the front. Several windows lined the walls, pouring light into the space. At the back of the library was a multimedia section separated from the rest of the room. "What will I be doing here?"

Mrs. Conrad smiled. "I promise it'll be relatively painless. You'll be helping me organize some things, assisting patrons, running small errands. Is that okay with you?"

"According to my mom, it is."

Laughter bubbled out of her. It wasn't unpleasant. Viktor's nerves relaxed a bit. Maybe this wouldn't be so bad after all.

Picking up a couple of books from a nearby stack, she

said, "Come on. I'll show you the ropes."

About forty minutes later, Viktor knew where fiction and nonfiction were shelved, how to access the internet, where the restrooms were located, and what to do if confronted by an unruly patron (i.e., call for Mrs. Conrad).

Distracting Viktor from those thoughts, though, were Janie Brooks and Celeste McDowell, who were entering the library just a few yards in front of him. Great. Just what he needed.

He watched the girls as they disappeared down the horror aisle. Surprise filled him at their choice, and he couldn't help but wonder what Celeste might find scary. Ghosts? Zombies? Bigfoot's older brother, Carl? Nope, Viktor thought. It had to be a mirror. But a magic one. One that would reflect the ugliness of her soul.

"Friends of yours?" Mrs. Conrad said, picking up her coffee mug and following his eyes to the two girls.

Viktor shrugged. "If by friends you mean archenemy and her bestie, then yeah."

"Ah." Mrs. Conrad nodded. "Let's put these books away, and then afterward I'll show you how to check books out to people. Sound good?"

"Yeah." Viktor flicked another glance back to where he'd last seen the girls. "I guess so."

"It's not so bad, trust me," she said, looking at the clock above the front doors. "Oh, shoot. It's almost time for the bell to ring. Bring your muscles tomorrow. We've got some heavy lifting to do. See those boxes by the door? We just got a delivery of a bunch of copies of *Dracula* for Mrs. Harkins's classes, and I could use the extra hands unboxing and delivering them to her classroom."

"Not a problem. As a matter of fact, I need a copy for that class."

"Feel free to grab one on your way out. We can make it library official tomorrow." She smiled.

"Cool. But just so you know, Mrs. Harkins is out sick. The sub is Mrs. McMillan, but she said we can call her October."

"Oh, that's nice." She smiled again, and not at all in a thanks-for-the-useless-information way. "It's a great book. Have you read it yet?"

"I'm . . . not much of a reader." He shrugged, waiting for her to give him a list of reasons why he should give reading a chance. It was almost like book nerds had memorized the same script and used it whenever they encountered someone who preferred an extracurricular activity that was anything but devouring words on a page.

"I see. Well . . . challenge accepted." She beamed but dropped the subject without adding even an ounce of guilt. "See you tomorrow, Viktor. And thanks for your help today!"

Viktor nodded and slipped his messenger bag over his head. All in all, it hadn't been the worst time of his life, that was for sure. The work had been interesting, Mrs. Conrad had been pretty cool, and even Celeste's presence hadn't made his head throb with irritation. Maybe it wouldn't be so bad helping at the library this year.

The rest of the day flew by like it didn't even happen, and just as the final bell rang, Viktor's phone buzzed to life with a text from his mom.

Mom: Would you mind picking up a bag of burgers and fries on your way home for dinner?

Viktor: Can I get a strawberry shake?

Mom: Bring one for your sister. 😀

Viktor: I guess.

Mom: Thank you, Viktor. The day's gotten away from me and this will help me out in a big way. I'll put money on your card. Be safe coming home.

She always told him that—to be safe. Whether he was leaving the house or headed back there, it was something you could set your watch to. Did Mom actually think that Nowhere was such a dangerous place? The town hosted a firefly festival every year. The police patrol car had a bumper sticker on it that read "wee-woo." The place couldn't get any more charming or safe if it tried.

After exchanging a few books at his locker, Viktor moved out the school door, heading south, toward Main Street. The Tasty Cow wasn't the best diner in the world, but it was the best in downtown Nowhere. While most of the town was what could only be described as "obnoxiously quaint," the Tasty Cow could really only be described as "sore-thumb chic." Hanging in each of its windows were neon signs that looked like glowing menu items—burgers, fries, drinks. The glass of the door was covered in stickers about shopping local and supporting the farmers of Nowhere and the surrounding area, and the corkboard hanging beside the front counter featured flyers advertising concerts in nearby cities that Viktor would never be able to attend and events around town that Viktor couldn't care less about. But the burgers . . . they were super delicious, despite the fact that if you weren't careful, half of one would end up in your lap. If you were careful, on the other hand, only a quarter of it would. They were messy, but delicious, and pretty much the sole thing Viktor ever ordered there, except for fries.

"Welcome to the Tasty Cow." The older blond lady behind the counter greeted him with a warm smile before picking up a pen and pad of paper. "What can I get you?"

Viktor looked at the menu, even though he didn't need to, and wondered why he'd made a habit of doing so. "Can I get three Sloppy King Jr.'s—two of them medium rare—four Sloppy fries, two medium strawberry shakes, and a Coronary Special with extra onion rings on it?"

After jotting down his order, the lady winked at him, like they shared some secret he wasn't aware of. "You got it, sweetie."

As Viktor waited, he scanned the diner for any familiar faces, but found none that he cared to say hi to—not that many people fell into that category, anyway. But sitting in the corner booth was a family he didn't recognize. He wondered if they were the new neighbors, but then mentally slapped himself for being stupid. Of course they were. People didn't come through Nowhere—it was on the way to nothing. There was nothing to attract tourists to the little town. They didn't even have a world's biggest ball of anything. So why were they here?

The person he presumed to be the mom was lean and delicate-looking, but with sharp eyes that seemed to take in every iota of her surroundings in detail with just a glance. The man next to her was broad-shouldered, with hands that said he'd been working hard all of his life. Beside him sat the girl who had waved to Viktor through the window—the girl who kept popping into his thoughts without rhyme or reason. Her eyes were as green as a moss-covered riverbank, her skin pale as the moon—all but for the light sprinkling of freckles across her nose. Tiny stars on her moonlike skin. When she glanced toward Viktor and the corners of her mouth lifted some in a small smile, his breath caught in his throat for a moment.

"Here ya go, kiddo."

"Hmm?" He turned back to the woman at the counter, who'd noticed that he'd noticed the new girl. As she handed him a brown paper sack and the drinks, she gave him a knowing look. He cleared his throat and managed a small "thanks" before heading out the door. On his way home, he thought about the girl and why she'd waved at some stranger in a strange town in the middle of the night, but he didn't focus on it for long.

The walk home from his after-school stop seemed a lot longer than it had last year. Viktor suspected that was due to a beautiful, still-summer day being sucked down the drain, leaving him a hollow husk, thirsting for any semblance of fun. Of course, as much as he was loathe to admit it . . . his first day back at school hadn't been all bad. It turned out that October, and therefore the English class, had been super cool. Mrs. Conrad was pretty funny, and he'd been all but invisible to Celeste the entire day. But no matter how not-terrible his first day had been, Viktor was just happy to be going home.

By the time he reached his front door, he'd already developed a plan of attack for the rest of the evening, so that he might salvage at least a little bit of his day. His plan was simple: consume five tons of junk food, suck down a million cans of caffeinated soda, and kill off as many virtual vampires as possible. Then—and only then—did he plan to crack open the copy of *Dracula* that Mrs. Conrad let him check out and see what the big fuss was.

As he stepped up on his porch, his head filled with the promise of sugar and gore, a voice spoke up from behind him. "Hello there."

He gasped and turned around to find the new girl from across the street standing on the sidewalk, smiling at him.

His tongue felt like it was swelling up inside his mouth, almost choking him. "H-hi . . ."

"I just moved in across the street. You're Viktor, right?" Her eyes sparkled in a way that outshone any girl he'd ever met. It might have had something to do with the fact that she was speaking to him when she didn't have to, but he wasn't sure. She held her head up with confidence. And when she smiled, Viktor wondered why, of all the places that she could be at that moment, she was standing in front of his house, talking to him. Across the street, the people he presumed were her parents were exiting their car. They must have left the Tasty Cow right after he did, and he hadn't noticed.

His mouth was so dry it felt like he'd swallowed sand. "Yeah . . . h-how did you know?"

She shrugged. "Small town. People talk. You know."

"Yeah. Do . . ." He glanced both ways down the street, still baffled at her presence. "Do you need help with something?"

"Nope. Just wanted to say hi and introduce myself. My family moved here from California, so we're still getting settled."

"Oh." Say hi? To him? "Well, hi, then."

A small laugh escaped her, followed by a smirk that fell on her cupid's-bow lips. "Are you always this chatty?"

His face grew hot. He could only hope he wasn't blushing as bad as he knew he must be. "Sorry."

"Don't be. I like quirky people, and I bet you're my kind of weird." She tilted her head a bit to the side, beaming. "Anyway, I was supposed to start school today, but something got messed up with my paperwork, so I'll start tomorrow. See you there?"

"Yeah."

"Oh," she said, throwing a smile over her shoulder at him as she walked away. "By the way . . . I'm Alys."

He watched her as she crossed the street to her house. When she reached her door, she turned and offered him a wave. Under his breath and to himself, Viktor said, "Totally."

Viktor proceeded to melt into a twelve-year-old puddle of goo.

The house was quiet when he stepped inside, which didn't surprise him. Dad wouldn't return for quite a while and Hannah wouldn't be home from school for another hour. Viktor's throat still felt like a desert, so he moved into the kitchen for a drink, but stopped short when he reached the archway leading into it.

Hanging over the edge of the sink was a shirtsleeve, which wouldn't have bothered him at all. But it was spattered with big spots of deep crimson. It looked like blood.

"What the . . . ?" he mumbled, as his head swam. He hated the sight of blood. So much so that he fainted on the regular whenever he had to have blood drawn or when Hannah scraped her knee. His feet felt like they were made of cement as he forced himself to cross the room to the sink. It was full of water, and standing closer, he could see that the water was a burgundy color. It smelled like rotten pennies. Somebody had been bleeding. A lot.

"Mom?!" he shouted, hurrying back to the living room to put some distance between him and the bloody sink. His heart hammered inside his chest. His lungs felt like someone was squeezing them so tight he couldn't breathe. He was proud of himself for not passing out, but he imagined he was still standing upright due only to his adrenaline skyrocketing from fear that someone that he loved had been injured.

What could have happened? Had Mom fallen on a kitchen knife while preparing lunch? Had Dad had an accident with a power tool? Was it Hannah who'd been hurt? His heart was racing, filling his ears with a whooshing sound. "Mom, are you home?!"

"Yes, Viktor. Just putting away some laundry," she called from upstairs. "How was your first day as a seventh grader? Good to know you survived."

As his mom came down the stairs, he said, "Are you okay?"

"I'm fine, dear, why?"

He threw an arm in the direction of the kitchen. How could she be so calm when it looked like someone had been murdered? "There's a pile of bloody clothes in the sink! Who got hurt? Is it Hannah? Or Dad? Are they okay?"

Mom gave him that calming look that she always gave him whenever he was freaking out about something that didn't need freaking out over. "Calm down, Viktor. I just had a little accident at the blood drive today. I'm soaking my clothes to get the stains out before I throw them in the washer. That's all."

His heart began to ease up on its marathon, but his nerves were still on absolute edge. His stomach was starting to hurt—something that happened whenever he was stressed out. Viktor furrowed his brow, recalling in his mind's eye the horror show in the sink. He still felt the threat of fainting coursing through his body "It's an awful lot of blood, Mom. What happened? You hit some guy's artery or what?"

As she made her way past him to the kitchen, she chuckled. "You could say that."

Once his lungs could take in air okay again, he followed her back to the kitchen and said, "You gotta be more careful. That scared the crap outta me."

Pulling the plug from the sink, she started draining the basin and wringing excess water from her shirt with her hands. "Sorry about that. How was your first day, anyway?"

"It was okay, I guess. Better than expected." Viktor shrugged as he set the bag of burgers on the counter and hung his messenger bag off the back of one of the dining chairs. He averted his eyes from what Mom was doing and tried to force the threat of nausea back down his throat.

"I know what I said earlier, but truth be told, I'm not very hungry now, and your father mentioned grabbing a bite to eat on his way home." She smiled to herself before asking,

"Why don't you clean up and grab one of the burgers you brought home for dinner?"

"If you don't mind, I'll wait a few minutes first." As he opened the window to air the kitchen out, Viktor said, "Oh, by the way, I met one of the new neighbors."

Mom's hands tightened on the shirt she was holding, but this time in tension. Viktor couldn't see her face from where he was standing, but every inch of her seemed on edge. Three heartbeats passed before she said, "Oh? I can't wait to hear everything about them."

CHAPTER SEVEN
The Pursuit of Impossible Things

"He noticed you." The man joined her at the window, following her gaze. She was looking at the boy's house again.

The girl shrugged in mock confidence. "Of course he did. I'm good at my job."

From the corner of her eye, she could see his jaw twitch. "Arrogance is unbecoming of a Slayer."

Brushing off his criticism, she straightened her shoulders and said, "What would you say is the most important trait a Slayer can have?"

"A good Slayer?" His eyebrow raised. They both knew he wasn't inquiring what kind of Slayer they were talking about. He was reminding her of her past mistakes, wordlessly whispering into her psyche, "I will never forget your failures." She managed a nod in response, but she was having a hard time stopping her bottom lip from trembling. Would she or her actions ever be enough for him?

"There is a singular trait that matters in a good Slayer." He placed a firm hand on her shoulder and, giving it a squeeze, bent down and spoke into her ear with a soft tone. "Follow-through."

And with that, the girl had her answer.

No.

It didn't matter how many vampires she killed or how well she maintained her 4.0 GPA. All that she was and could offer would never be enough for her father.

And the real kicker was that even knowing so wasn't enough to crush the desire to pursue it.

CHAPTER EIGHT
A Moment of Tension

Viktor sat on his balcony, smelling his mom's prize-winning roses below and admiring the stars above. The air outside was warm that night. He'd closed *Dracula* just an hour earlier, when Damon had texted to say his mom had changed her mind about the spaghetti and bonding and he'd be "right over," but had picked it up again when, surprise surprise, Damon was a no-show. The book, so far, was decent. It was about a young lawyer guy who was hired by this wealthy count dude named Dracula to handle some legal stuff, and when he goes to Transylvania to do the job he was hired for, things get weird. Like vampire weird. Like, this poor lawyer had no idea the supernatural weirdness that would be waiting there for him.

The story was good enough that Viktor found himself

thinking about opening it back up again moments after shutting the cover. But then, at long last, Damon appeared from around the corner and waved. Viktor headed back inside to greet him, book in hand.

Mom and Dad were in the living room and there was a distinct tension in the air, as if they'd been engaged in a pretty serious conversation before Viktor walked in. He stopped in his tracks. "Everything okay, guys?"

There was a long pause before Dad said, "Everything's fine, Viktor. Your mother tells me you met the new neighbors."

An odd feeling settled in Viktor's stomach. "Yeah. Well, I mean, just one of them. The daughter. Her name is Alys. She seems nice. Why?"

Dad cleared his throat and drummed his fingers on the arm of his chair before speaking again. "Did she say why they chose to move to Nowhere, by chance?"

"Nope. She pretty much just said hi and mentioned they moved here from California." Viktor furrowed his brow. "Is something wrong?"

"No. It was just a long day at the office, kiddo," Dad said. His parents exchanged looks then, which weirded him out even more. After a moment, Dad glanced at the book in Viktor's hand. "What are you reading, son?"

"Oh. It's *Dracula*, for my English class. We're doing a creative writing assignment on what it would be like for a vampire to live in modern times."

Dad nodded, his forehead creased. "It would be a challenge in more ways than one, I'm sure."

Viktor tilted his head some in concern. He was about to give voice to it, but then his dad switched gears and got that obnoxious gleam in his eyes again. "Hey, did I tell you I'm reading a book about antigravity?"

Viktor released a presumptive groan. "No . . ."

Dad grinned, holding back his laughter at his terrible joke before he even revealed the punch line. "Yeah, it's impossible to put down."

Viktor rolled his eyes and looked at Mom. "He just can't help himself, can he?"

"I actually own a very old copy of the book you're reading, Viktor. Let me see if I . . ." Standing, he scanned the bookcase for a moment before plucking a book from its shelves. He ran a hand lovingly over the yellow cover before handing it to Viktor. "Ahh! Here we are. I haven't read it in a very long time, but I recall it being entertaining."

Viktor turned the book over in his hands. It was funny how different antique books felt compared to their modern counterparts. He always thought they felt heavier, somehow. He flipped open the cover, and written on the inside in ornate, swirling script were the words "For you, my friend, and in ways, for all of Elysia. In Brotherhood, Vikas."

There was a knock on the door and Mom's eyes shot to it. When she spoke, Viktor was almost certain that her voice shook a little. "I wonder who that might be."

"Oh, I forgot to tell you. Damon's coming over. I mean . . . I guess he's already over." Viktor shrugged as he handed the book back to his dad and headed for the front door, leaving the weird interaction with his parents behind for the moment. He opened the door to Damon, who was just then removing the buds from his ears. "Hey man."

"'Sup?"

"Dude, this is Nowhere. Nothing is ever up." Damon cast him a woeful look.

"True," Viktor said. "Come on. Let's hang out upstairs."

When they reached Viktor's bedroom, Damon raised his eyebrow in that typical Damon way. "No snacks?"

Viktor thought about it for about 0.25 seconds before he replied, "I'll go grab chips and soda. Want some chocolate too?"

Damon rolled his eyes, as if Viktor's question was the dumbest thing ever asked. "Of course I do."

As Viktor descended the stairs once again with visions of junk food filling every corner of his mind, he heard his parents' lowered voices, dripping with tension.

Mom's tone had a tinge of sadness to it. "I can't believe it's going to end like this, Drake."

"We have no other choice, my love." There was a long pause, and then Dad's voice chimed in with an undertone of anger. "If I have to kill him myself, I will."

The tiny hairs on the back of Viktor's neck stood on end. His steps slowed.

There was no way he'd heard his dad say that. His dad wouldn't hurt a fly.

Would he?

Of course not. Dad had to be exaggerating over being upset with someone. That had to be it. If he'd said that in the first place, that is, and maybe Viktor had just misconstrued what his dad had said.

Mom and Dad glanced at Viktor as he made his way into the room. Viktor said, "I was, um, just getting some snacks."

His parents exchanged looks that said they realized he'd overheard them, but they said nothing. They waited for him to leave. Which just added to the weirdness of the moment.

After a brief pause, Viktor carried all his worries and brand-new fears into the kitchen in search of something sweet to counter the strange bitterness that had brushed his soul.

Even once he'd collected snacks for himself and Damon and had returned to his room, he still felt distracted by the weird interaction with his mom and dad, but he wasn't sure why it bugged him so much. Adults were weird. Parents were even weirder. It was just a fact of life.

Damon sighed. "Could you focus for a second? I'm trying to show you something."

It wasn't easy, but Viktor pulled his attention from his bedroom door and turned back to Damon. "Sorry. What did you wanna show me, anyway?"

"I could've just sent you a screenshot, but I wanted to see

the look on your face when I showed this to you." Pulling out his phone from his pocket, Damon searched for a particular text message. "I was on a group text with Taylor, Drew, and Janie, and we were talking about this back-to-school party that Taylor's planning for Thursday, since we have Friday off for that stupid teachers-in-service thing. I mentioned bringing you, and Janie said she didn't think it was a good idea. But then Taylor said this."

Beaming, Damon thrust the phone into Viktor's hands. "Go on. Look."

Still distracted, Viktor took the phone and read Taylor's response. I dunno. He seems okay to me. He should come.

He read it over again . . . and again, trying to wrap his head around why Damon thought he needed to see it. "I . . . what does that mean?"

"Dude. Can't you read?" Damon rolled his eyes. "It means that maybe you're not the social pariah you always seem to make yourself out to be. People want you at the party."

Viktor raised a suspicious eyebrow. "Are you sure he knew he was talking about me?"

"As opposed to another Viktor?" Damon sighed, shaking his head. "We've gotta work on your self-esteem, bro."

Viktor handed his phone back. "My self-esteem is just fine, thanks."

"Mm-hmm." After returning his phone to his pocket, Damon said, "So, about this party . . ."

Viktor's eyes widened. His throat was starting to feel dry

again, which made him wonder if it was a sign of stress or if he needed Mom to pick him up some of those throat-soothing lozenges. "I can't go to a party."

"Why not? Got some big plans for this weekend that I'm not aware of?" It was Damon's turn to raise an eyebrow. "Look. Come to the party. It'll be fun. I'll make sure of it. And if it's not, we'll leave. No big deal. Cool?"

Viktor considered his options. He could either hang out at some party with Damon . . . or he could stay home and play *Pinkie's Big Adventure* on the Xbox with Hannah all night. "Yeah. I mean, I guess. We'll see how I feel on Friday."

"Good. Now that we've got that settled, what do you say we kill a vampire or two or a zillion before I head home? Or are you scared that big guy will beat you again?"

"I'm not scared." His eyes once more found his bedroom door and an ache filled his center as his mind flicked to what he thought he'd heard his dad say. "Not of that," he mumbled.

CHAPTER NINE
Ketchup and Coffins

Viktor wasn't sure why he'd gotten to his first class so early the next morning, but when he arrived, he couldn't help but notice that he was alone. That is, until October walked through the door, balancing a stack of papers in one hand and a cup of coffee in the other. When she saw Viktor, she smiled. "Hey, Viktor. How's it going?"

"Not bad, I guess. I started reading *Dracula* last night." Just saying the words aloud made him rethink them. It was so unlike him to pick up a book and just read it, but *Dracula* was pretty good.

"Yeah? That's great! What do you think so far?"

"It's . . . weird. But, like . . . good-weird, I think." He cringed at how awkward he thought he sounded. "Does that make any sense?"

"Trust me. If anyone knows something about something being good-weird, it's yours truly." They chuckled together.

"I'm liking it so far, so thanks for the assignment. Less boring that a lot of the stuff Mrs. Harkins was rumored to assign," Viktor said. "So, are you, like, really into vampire stories then, or . . . ?"

"Oh yeah, big time. You name a piece of vampire fiction written in the last two hundred years, and I've read it." A curious smile lifted the corner of her burgundy-painted lips. For a moment, she seemed bemused by some private thought. "Devoured it, one might say."

Everything about October's aesthetic screamed *goth*, but there was something else about her that Viktor couldn't put his finger on. Something darker. Otherworldly. But then, maybe it was just the goth thing he was picking up on. He didn't know many goths in Nowhere—in fact, he didn't know any personally at all. Still, whatever it was about her was strange. And intriguing. "When did you get into the genre?"

"Oh, I was a bit younger than you when I started reading it obsessively. But my fixation really took a deep dive after high school. Some events in my life took a turn that really pointed hard-core at all things fangs and blood and bats and gore." The look in her eye suggested she was somewhere else for a moment, reliving a time in her life, perhaps, that their conversation had stirred up. When she came back to the moment, she said, "What about you? Does any subject matter call to you like that?"

"Not really. I mean . . ." Viktor sighed. "To be honest, I've never been a big reader. But *Dracula* is pretty good so far."

"I'm quite certain you'll eat it up." The first bell rang, interrupting their conversation. "Looks like it's about that time. Would you mind grabbing the books Mrs. Conrad is holding in the library so the rest of the class can catch up?"

"Sure."

She smiled as the rest of the class filed into the room. "Hurry back, 'kay?"

The library was busy by the time Viktor arrived, which didn't seem normal for school mornings. Mrs. Conrad was buzzing about, helping students, and while most people might feel overwhelmed at the number of tasks she had laid out before her, Mrs. Conrad looked happier than Viktor thought anyone inside a library had ever looked. The moment she noticed him her eyes lit up. "Viktor! So glad you're here. Please take those boxes to Mrs. McMillan's class, would you? After you unload the books, you can bring the cart back here."

"Not a problem."

Viktor pulled the cart through the open library doors and back down the hall to English class. He kind of loved being in the hall during class. For one, almost no people were there. For two, even though he was always sure to get a hall pass first, it always felt a little like he was breaking the rules. At least to the level that Viktor was comfortable breaking the rules.

Pulling open the door to his class, Viktor managed to push the full cart into the room with a grunt. The boxes retaliated by flinging one of the books to the ground with a thud. Several students chuckled. One in the back started a slow clap that nobody else joined in on or acknowledged. October helped Viktor pick up the book and then said, "I appreciate your help. Would you mind passing out a copy to every student? Then you can stack the rest of the boxes by the window."

Viktor nodded and got to work. Once every kid in his class had a copy of the book, October announced that the rest of the hour would be for quiet reading. Viktor found himself rushing to get the remaining boxes unloaded and then rushing again to return the cart to the library, just so he could find out what other horrors were awaiting Dracula's lawyer, Mr. Jonathan Harker. It was a strange thing, being interested in a book, but Viktor was just rolling with it. If he was going to read, it was going to be about something cool, like vampires.

The irony that he was enjoying a book about a creature who subsisted on human blood when he himself couldn't handle the sight of a paper cut without feeling woozy was not lost on him. But the story was solid. The main character, Jonathan Harker, felt lost and confused—a feeling that really resonated with Viktor. The characters Mina and Lucy reminded him of his own aunts. And all the spooky stuff was just cool. So it was no wonder that the story chased him throughout the day. It had cast its spell on him. Kinda like the way that Dracula had cast his spell over so many people in the book.

His morning flew by after that and before Viktor knew it, he was walking into the library for the third time that day. After a brief hello, Mrs. Conrad put Viktor on front-desk duty to check books out to people.

"You don't mind, do you?" she asked, her glasses poised on the tip of her nose, a pencil behind her ear.

There was no way Viktor felt ready to run the front desk by himself, but there was also no way he was going to allow for the remote possibility of Mrs. Conrad calling his mom to complain about his lack of dedication. "Nope. It's all good."

As she hurried away to assist a boy who seemed to be wandering aimlessly between the cooking and art sections, she exclaimed over her shoulder, "Just scream if you need me!"

"Okay, Mrs. Conrad." Viktor looked around. A pile of books that needed to be returned to the shelves was sitting on the desk. Picking them up in one fell swoop, he marveled at how heavy books could be. Like, they were just paper and cardboard. What kind of glue were they using to make these things? *They're probably heavy because they used cement . . . rubber cement*, he thought, chuckling to himself. On the heels of that chuckle was the mortifying realization that his dad would love that joke.

Shaking his head, he bent down to sit the books on the floor beside the already full cart, and the moment he did, he heard a girl's voice from the other side of the desk.

"Excuse me. I'd like to check out this book, please."

Standing in front of him, wearing all black, which made her look a bit like a redheaded Wednesday Addams, was his new neighbor. She was wearing a small smile that bloomed a bit when she looked into his eyes—an act so sweet, so endearing . . . it almost made Viktor vomit from nervousness. She placed a book on the counter and tilted her head to the side, as if trying to gauge his reaction.

After time stretched on for eons, he managed to say, "Um. Yeah. I can do that for you."

"Thanks. That would be awfully neighborly of you." She beamed.

He took the book from her and tried not to fret about his awkward greeting or how stupid he sounded or how dumb his white splotch of hair must look, and a million other things that he hoped she wouldn't notice. "*Dracula*, huh? I'm reading this for Mrs. McMillan's class."

"Well, I'm grateful for the friendly face. Some people . . ." She flicked her eyes to Celeste, who was passing by the open library doors. "Some haven't been as nice as you."

"Ugh. That's Celeste. She's a jerk. Ignore her. That's what I do." He flipped open the cover to reveal the barcode, so he could scan it. "What's your name?"

"Alys. A-l-y-s."

His cheeks ached from smiling so much. "Like the Wonderland story?"

"Kinda."

"Do you have your student ID yet?"

"Oh. Yeah."

After he scanned her ID to fill out the form on the computer with stuff like her name (Alys—he knew because he'd repeated it to himself a million times since she'd shared it with him), address (close enough to his house that he thought about her whenever he glanced at a window), and phone number (which she'd never give to a dork like him), he said, "Have you read it?"

"Yeah, a couple of times, but if Mrs. McMillan's going to force us all to write essays on it, I figured I should dust off my brain cobwebs and give it another go. She ran out of copies and said I could get one here."

"What did you think of it?"

"I like the writing style, how it's all letters and journal entries. That was a pretty neat way to present the story. Oh, and I thought the brides were pretty messed up, for sure. But yeah. It's a good book." Her sparkling eyes lit up with a question. "Can I ask why you volunteer here? Are you a big book nerd or something?"

"Um. No. Not exactly."

"Oh." She shrugged. "That's a shame. Because I am."

"You're a book nerd?" Perfect, Viktor. You're a genius.

It's a wonder all the ladies aren't clamoring for your phone number.

Shifting his feet, Viktor became a little worried he might have hurt her feelings with what he'd just said.

"A hundred and fifty percent. And proud of it." She beamed. "So if you're not a book nerd, why do you volunteer here?"

Viktor shrugged. "My mom thought I needed something to do all school year that isn't . . . you know . . . fun."

Alys rolled her eyes in empathy. "Some parents suck. They can be so annoying."

"Tell me about it."

She said, "Have you started it yet? *Dracula*, I mean."

"Yeah, but it's . . . long. And reading's not really my thing, so it may take me a while. I like it so far, though."

She smiled. "Who do you relate to more? Dracula, the vampire? Or Van Helsing, the vampire Slayer?"

"So far, I think I can relate to Jonathan Harker more than either of them." He handed her ID back to her and said, "He was just this dude, trying to live his life, and then he gets all mixed up in something he never wanted to do, but knew he had no choice. Ya know?"

She took the ID and as she slipped it inside her pants pocket, she said, "Wow. I guess I never thought about Harker much before. What makes you feel that way?"

Viktor sighed. "I dunno. Maybe because everyone in the world seems to have firm opinions on what I should be doing but me."

"Hmm. Maybe you're not Jonathan Harker. Maybe you're some side character we don't notice in the book. Like . . . the carriage driver that took Harker to Dracula's castle. Maybe he was a sweet guy who had a hard time talking to girls until he had to check a book out to one at the middle school library." She winked at him, and in that moment, Viktor was pretty certain that he had either fallen deep into a dream or died.

"I . . . um . . ." He wasn't sure what he should say to that.

She tilted her head to the side a little, looking like she was kind of charmed by him, and said, "Do you wanna split a plate of fries after school?"

Words still escaping him, Viktor nodded and handed her the book. "I . . . yeah! I'd like that."

"Great!" As she tucked the book under her arm, she smiled and said, "I'll see you at the Tasty Cow at three o'clock. It'll be you, me, and enough fries to choke a wolf."

"Cool," he said, his voice a little shaky. Girls never talk to him. They barely looked at him, and didn't often notice that he existed. Being asked to hang out by someone like . . .

He breathed her name aloud with a wistful sigh. "Alys."

Like Alys in Wonderland, where that girl chased a rabbit into a . . . rose garden, he thought, full of . . . clams, maybe? Viktor shook his head. He really needed to read more.

He made a mental note to read more *Dracula* tonight when he got home.

If nothing else, it would give him and Alys more to talk about . . . which could only be a good thing.

* * *

When the clock read 2:57, Viktor readied himself for the wailing bell that signified the end of the school day—and the time to hang out with Alys. She really seemed to maybe like him a little, if Viktor was reading things right.

He probably wasn't.

That didn't mean she didn't like him; he'd just always had a difficult time interpreting people's intention toward him. Maybe something in his brain had gotten screwed up by Celeste's nonstop bullying. Regardless, he had a hard time trusting other people, and an even harder time trusting his own instincts. Alys seemed so confident and nice, and just the thought of her wanting to spend time with him—even just as friends—was enough to make Viktor's heart swell up to the size of a watermelon.

Beside him, Damon appeared and opened his locker with a huff. "Bro, if Mrs. Lapinsky doesn't let me bake and decorate a cake during Food and Nutrition class this semester, I'm going to lose it."

Viktor chuckled. "You do know that bingeing hours of British baking shows doesn't make you a chef, right? Or whatever a cake maker is called."

"Baker. And if today proved anything, it's that I'm the only person in that class who understands and appreciates the difference between fondant and modeling chocolate." After a brief pause, Damon shrugged. "I'm just saying."

Viktor cleared his throat. "Hey man, I've gotta run an

errand on my way home, so you're on your own for the afternoon, okay?"

"An errand?" Damon raised an eyebrow at him. "What errand?"

"I'll tell you about it later. Promise." It wasn't that he wanted to keep his meetup with Alys secret or anything. He just wanted to keep that moment for himself for a little while.

"Okay, man. Don't do anything I wouldn't do."

After closing his locker, Viktor stepped outside the school and made his way toward the Tasty Cow. As he drew closer, his head began to fill with doubt. What if it was all a joke? What if Alys was just pulling a prank on her dorky new neighbor, and didn't plan to be there at all? Or, even worse, what if she was just meeting up with him out of pity?

As he stepped inside the diner, he held his breath and looked around at the tables and booths, shrinking a bit at every face that wasn't hers, every chair that sat empty. Then, drawing his attention to a booth on the far wall, was Alys, waving at him, wearing the same warm smile she'd been wearing earlier that day in the library.

Viktor's lungs released the breath he'd been holding in a relieved, albeit nervous, sigh. Maybe it was real after all.

As he crossed the room, Viktor's feet felt heavier and heavier, until he began to wonder if gravity was clinging to his ankles, as if pleading with him to stop what he was doing and run. Run away so quick and so fast that no one would even remember he'd been there. *Stupid gravity*, he thought. *Not now. Be gravity-ish later.*

"Hey there," Alys said as he approached the booth. "How was the rest of your day?"

"Nothing exciting," he said, sliding into the seat across from her. He placed his book on the seat beside him. "Just people I don't wanna see and stuff I don't wanna do. You know."

The restaurant was filling up. He wondered if Damon might come in and see him there, talking to a pretty stranger. He hoped so. Because there was no way that Damon would ever believe it when Viktor told him.

The blond lady who had helped Viktor out at the counter the day before sashayed over with a notepad and pen. "What can I get you two?"

"A monster plate of fries and two sodas?" As he spoke the last word in a questioning tone, he glanced at Alys, who nodded her agreement.

"You've got it. Coming right up." As the waitress left, she gave Viktor's shoulder a squeeze. He wasn't sure why. Maybe she was just acknowledging that she remembered him from yesterday? Maybe she was just being nice?

Viktor looked at Alys. He kept flicking his gaze away, so she wouldn't think he was staring at her. Even though he was 100 percent staring at her.

He cleared his throat. "So, what about you? How was your first day at school?"

Alys chuckled, rolling her eyes. "Geez, Viktor. You might as well ask me about the weather. It was fine. Typical first day of school. Ask me something more . . . personal."

Like what? Viktor thought. His tongue felt like it was made of lead. "Um . . . okay. Why did you move here?"

Something dark passed over her eyes—dark enough and for long enough that it both got Viktor's attention and made him wonder what the story was behind it.

"My family just needed a change. The last place we lived wasn't the best for us. A lot of stress. My dad's job was putting him through the ringer without enough reward. So . . . we came to Nowhere. To start a new life and resolve some family stuff." She smiled again, but it was forced. Viktor wondered if he'd ruined the moment. But then her smile lightened, and she said, "Good enough answer for ya?"

"Totally." It was Viktor's turn to smile. He hoped she saw the support and understanding in it that he was trying to express. Maybe she wouldn't. Maybe she'd just see a guy who had never sat alone in a booth with a girl sharing a plate of fries and asking personal questions before smiling at her because he had no idea what else to do. She wouldn't be wrong about that—not at all. He said, "You can ask me anything too, ya know."

"Okay. Hmm . . . let me see . . ." She looked up for a moment, as if all the right questions were written on the ceiling. "What about *your* parents? What are they like?"

"They're . . . well . . ." He shrugged. "They're pretty

boring, to be honest. Mom is the director of this charity helping girls who've been orphaned or abandoned. Plus, she does volunteer work—a lot of it at the blood bank. Dad designs specialty and custom coffins for people around the world. They both drive me crazy about keeping my grades up. You know. Pretty much normal parents, I guess."

The waitress set a plate of fries on the table along with two sodas. The fries smelled amazing, and Viktor's mouth was already watering.

"Your dad designs coffins?" She leaned forward, very interested in what he had to say. "That's pretty cool."

"Yeah. I mean, I guess." He shrugged, popping a fry into his mouth. "He's got this weird thing about them being comfortable enough for a living person. I mean . . . as if dead people are in a position to complain."

"I know, right?" She picked up a fry and smeared it through the puddle of ketchup on the edge of the plate before biting off the end. "What kind of living creature would want to lie in a coffin?"

"Well," Viktor said, holding up his library book, "I can only think of one."

They both laughed together. It was a moment that seemed so organic and natural that Viktor started to worry a little bit less about why a girl, this girl, wanted to hang out with him.

After Viktor lay the book on the table between them, Alys traced her finger along its spine. "Do you ever think they might be . . . you know . . . real?"

"What? Vampires?" Viktor shook his head and chuckled. "There's no way. Something that bursts into flames in sunlight would never survive on Earth."

"Oh, I dunno. There are a lot of nocturnal creatures around. And what if the fictional stories just got the details a tiny bit wrong?" She shrugged, a playful smile dancing on her lips. "I'm just saying. There are crazier notions out there."

"Well, if vampires are real, I'll be sure to ask Mrs. McMillan. Because she's probably definitely one of them."

"What makes you say that?"

"I don't know. She's just . . . different." He picked up a fry and popped it into his mouth. After he chewed and swallowed, he said, "Don't get me wrong, I really like her. But she's a li'l spooky."

"Good to know. I'll have to keep my eye on her just in case she gets peckish." Her green eyes were sparkling.

"And while you're keeping an eye on her, I'd better keep my eye on you," he teased. "You're kinda on the spooky side as well, y'know."

Tilting her head to the side, she smiled. "Is that a bad thing?"

Viktor felt like he was dreaming. He held her gaze for a moment before responding. "Not even a little."

"I'm glad we did this, Viktor." The light in her eyes shone bright. "I think you and I are going to become good friends."

Viktor swallowed the huge lump in his throat that he was convinced might be his actual heart and wet his lips. It took every ounce of his bravery to say out loud what he was thinking with every cell of his being. "I . . . I'd like that."

More than anything, he thought.

CHAPTER TEN
Killing Time

Viktor couldn't believe it. Blood was everywhere. On the floor, the walls, the windows. Even on the clock on the wall that read 8:14 p.m. He hadn't been prepared for the absolute gore, but there it was, and he couldn't stop staring at it.

"Dude, get the one in the back of the room!" Damon was almost shouting.

Small beads of sweat dotted Viktor's forehead. His shoulders ached from being drawn up to his ears due to the tension of the situation. He knew that Damon's instructions were the only way out of this, but a big part of him worried that he wasn't good enough, that he'd never save them both, that he and Damon were about to die.

Out of nowhere, hands grabbed Damon's head, ripping it clear off his shoulders.

Damon set his controller down with a disappointed thud. "You let me die! All you had to do was kill the vampire at the back of the room and we'd have beat this level! But you let me die?!"

Viktor sighed, his shoulders slumping. "Sorry, man. I don't know why this level is so hard for me. Once we get in the house, I just freak out every time. There are so many vampires! And that big guy? He's unbeatable! I mean, how do the game developers expect anyone to advance in the game when this is in our way?"

"Don't worry about it. You'll figure it out." Damon slapped Viktor on the back. "But next time . . . you take point. I'm not getting my head ripped off again."

Decapitation or not, it had been a long first week at school, and Viktor could think of no better way to wind down than a Friday night with his best friend and a game with an M rating for blood, gore, and violence. Even if he did suck at playing the game.

He started to make a mental note of how effective decapitation might be against vampires, but decided to write it down instead. Grabbing his notebook from his messenger bag, he scribbled "Ways to kill a vampire: 1. Decapitation?"

"What are you writing?"

"I'm starting a list of ways I can maybe get better at this stupid game."

Damon shook his head. "We don't have to play it, ya know."

"Yes, we do. I love it. I just suck at it." As Viktor turned off the game system and television, his stomach rumbled. Glancing at the clock, he could discern why. His usual dinnertime had passed over three hours ago. He picked up his phone and texted his mom: Hey, are we on our own for dinner or are you bringing something home?

It took a moment, but after a while, Mom texted back: Sorry, sweetie. Can you two just order something to eat? Something's come up and I'm going to be late getting home tonight."

Viktor: NP. Is it cool if Damon stays over?

Mom: As long as you pick up after yourselves, it is. I've gotta go now. Love you.

After slipping his phone back into his pocket, Viktor said, "So what do you wanna eat for dinner?"

"Parents abandoned you to fend for yourself foraging the wilds for sustenance again, eh?"

Viktor shrugged. It was no big deal. Though . . . he was getting tired of having takeout so much and *not* having Dad's chili. "Yeah, I guess. This past week's been busy for both of them. So . . . I dunno . . . pizza?"

"Burgers would be better."

Viktor sighed in relief and took his phone out again. After five p.m., the Tasty Cow delivered. And fast, which made his stomach grumble a little more quietly.

"So . . . since your mom and dad aren't gonna be home for a while, I'm guessing they won't notice you're gone later tonight?" He was wearing that sly look that he sometimes got whenever he was hinting at doing something that might get them into trouble.

Viktor shook his head. "No way, bro. I already told you. I'm not going to that party."

"You one hundred percent *are* going to the party," Damon muttered under his breath—but not so quiet that Viktor wouldn't hear him. "That Alys girl might be there."

Viktor considered the possibility. He doubted Alys would be there, but what if she was? He had such a good time with her the other afternoon and definitely wanted to hang out again. It had only been a few days since they met up in the Tasty Cow. Was that long enough to wait before he looked like some desperate loser? A defeated sigh escaped him. Damon was always pushing him just outside the limits of his comfort zone. Sometimes it made him crazy. Mostly, it just made his time with Damon both stressful . . . and a whole lotta fun. "Why is it so important to you that I go to some stupid party, anyway?"

"Because you're cooler than you think, and if you'd just go, other people will see it too." Damon was giving him a look that said that he meant business. "Plus, you need more friends, especially if we want to rule the school in eighth grade. Now is the time to start."

Viktor paused before responding, because he needed Damon to hear the real reason that he didn't want to go to the party. "You mean because none of them see it now."

Damon met his eyes, his tone more serious than usual. "You know that's not what I meant."

"But that doesn't change the fact that none of your other friends like me. And it's okay if they don't. I don't need to have a million friends." And that was the truth. He needed one, two, maybe three that he could rely on to be there when he needed them to be. Damon was number one . . . and he guessed he'd meet number two and three someday. In the near future. Maybe Alys could be number two. If he ever got over being so awkward. "You don't have to stay here with me, you know. You could go to the party tonight. We can just hang out tomorrow or something. No big deal. For real."

Damon got quiet, and just as Viktor was about to ask him if he was okay, Damon nodded his head to some internal thought he was having and said, "Come on. Grab your shoes."

"What?" Viktor's eyes went wide. "No way. And we just ordered food. I'm not grabbing my—"

"Forget the food—we'll cancel the order. This is more important," Damon said. "Don't forget that I can pick you up and I will carry you. You wanna wear shoes to the party or not? Because you're going either way."

Viktor thought Damon might be serious. He had the strength and motive. But would he do it for real?

As if hearing Viktor's thoughts, Damon shrugged one shoulder. "Choice is yours."

* * *

A half hour later, Viktor was holding a plastic cup full of Mountain Dew and Skittles—Damon's personal recipe that he, of course, referred to as a "Damon Drink"—and watching the flames of the bonfire as people moved all around it. There were maybe twenty kids and one lone parent who was just trying to keep relative peace among the partygoers. Viktor recognized the man as Mr. Johnson. *Of course* it was Mr. Johnson. He was pretty sure this party was on the guy's property, and his son, David, was a pretty popular kid. Not Damon popular, but popular enough.

He was trying to figure out just what the point of a back-to-school party was. Gather a group of people around a bonfire and have them consume way too much sugar? It sounded just a little weird. But then, he was nervous, and no matter how many times Damon told him to relax, it didn't feel like he would be capable of relaxing ever again.

Maybe the party wasn't going to be so bad. Maybe he'd make a few friends and hang out with Alys again, if she showed up. It was already off to an okay start. He couldn't see Celeste anywhere.

"Hey Damon!" As if summoned by his thoughts, Celeste appeared on the opposite side of the bonfire and waved. Suddenly, Viktor felt smaller somehow.

"Uh, hey." Damon waved back with an air of nonchalance that said he couldn't care less that she was here.

Viktor grabbed him by the wrist. "I think . . . ," he

started, but it was too late to convince Damon that it was time to go. Celeste was walking over to them. Viktor shot Damon a look, but Damon didn't see it.

"There you are, Damon. I've been looking for you." Her voice was full of honey-dripping sunshine. It made Viktor's eyes roll just to hear it. "Are you having a good time?"

"Better than ever." Damon took in a mouthful of Damon Drink and swallowed.

"Oh, Viktor. You're here," she said flatly, as if she hadn't been looking at him just five seconds ago. Right away, to Viktor's relief, she turned her attention back to Damon. "I'm so glad you came. I was worried you might not make it."

"Trust your eyes. I made it," Damon said before turning his attention back to Viktor to say, "Y'know, this party is pretty boring after all. We should go."

"You're leaving already?" Celeste pouted. "Aren't you having fun? I was hoping you and I could talk."

She paused before looking at Viktor and adding, "Alone."

A small crease formed on Damon's forehead. He looked like he was thinking hard about something, but Viktor didn't have a chance to ask him what. Damon grabbed his sleeve and tugged him along after him. "Sorry, Celeste. Viktor and I, uh, have a thing we need to do."

Viktor let himself be tugged along but had no idea what Damon was talking about. Once the bonfire—and Celeste—were behind them, he said, "Remind me. What thing do we need to do?"

"I thought it was obvious. The thing we needed to do was to get away from Celeste."

Viktor smiled. "Y'know, man. There are several reasons you're my best friend. This is just one more of them."

"It's not only for your benefit, my dude. That girl has a crush on me, and I am so not here for it."

"Viktor!"

Turning around, Viktor couldn't help but smile when he saw Alys winding her way between small clusters of people and heading straight for him. He turned his attention back to Damon—or rather, he tried to, but Damon was suddenly missing in action. He should have been surprised, but the truth was, Damon had a lot of friends and shiny-object syndrome. It wasn't the first time his best friend had ditched him, and it wouldn't be the last.

Alys was smiling as she moved closer. "I thought that was you."

"Hey Alys." Viktor beamed. "How are you? Cool party, huh?"

She shrugged and didn't say a word in response, but her feelings were written plainly all over her face. She was looking very much like she didn't want to be here—just like him.

Viktor cleared his throat. "Hey, you wouldn't wanna get out of here, would you? Maybe I could walk you home or something?"

"And abandon the great joy of a middle school back-to-school party? Why would I want that?" The corner of her mouth twitched in teasing sarcasm.

The two of them wandered down a dirt path, away from the bonfire. The night air was cool, but not uncomfortably so. Just a hint of the autumn season that would soon be upon them. There was no sign of Damon, but Viktor didn't mind. Every step away from the music and talking and people was a step toward peace and quiet.

Alys seemed to enjoy the quiet as well, because when Viktor glanced over at her, she wore an expression of relief all over her face. Seeing it made him smile too.

"I had fun the other day at that diner with you," Alys said. "Thanks for being so nice to me. It's hard to move around a lot, y'know?"

"Yeah." He paused to consider his response. "I mean, no. I don't know. We moved here when I was a baby, and I haven't even left town many times since then."

"That sounds amazing."

"You think so?"

Alys nodded. "Having a home that you can count on as your go-to comfort zone? Knowing what lies around every corner and being able to rely on it being there from day to day? Oh yeah. It sounds like a dream."

The notion of somewhere like Nowhere being someone's idea of a dream just baffled him. "I guess that depends on your point of view. I know I could stand to live with a little excitement."

"Be careful, Viktor." Her steps slowed. She met his eyes

with a look of concern that sent a strange wave of curiosity over him. "Be careful what you wish for."

The air between them grew weird and full of something that Viktor could only describe as unsettled. They walked along in silence for a while. Viktor tried to think of a way to return the evening's vibe to fun and friendly, but it felt like he'd somehow ruined it, without even knowing how. After several minutes, the trail came to an end at the back of a cul-de-sac just down the street from where they each lived.

As they approached Alys's house, Viktor swallowed the lump in his throat and said, "Hey, we should . . ."

"We should what?"

"We should hang out more." After a nervous cough, he said, "Y'know?"

Alys visibly relaxed. Apparently, the tension he'd felt hadn't just been something he'd imagined. It dissipated, returning their evening to something good. "I think so too."

Viktor cleared his throat. "In case it's not super obvious, I don't have a ton of friends. I really just have Damon."

"That's not true." She shook her head. "You have me now too. I mean . . . if you want to be friends with me."

His smile felt so natural. Why was it so easy for him to smile whenever he was around her? "I think I'd like that."

"Y'know, truth be told . . ." She glanced around, as if she were about to share a secret with him and wanted to be certain nobody else would hear. "I've never really had friends."

"I find that hard to believe."

"We've always moved so much, I don't think I ever had time to make them. Growing up, I'd hang out with my cousins, but that's not the same." There was a sad glint in her eye. Viktor couldn't bear seeing it.

"Well, I'm glad we're friends."

She smiled, but the sadness was still there, just under the surface. "Me too."

"Anyway . . ." He toed the ground, trying to think of something cool and charming to say, but came up empty. "Have a good rest of your night."

"You too, Viktor Valentine." Beaming, she made her way up the steps and slipped inside her front door, but not before offering him a little wave that made his heart feel like an overfilled balloon.

As soon as Viktor walked through his front door, he nestled into the velvet Chesterfield sofa in the living room with his copy of *Dracula* and a soft chenille throw blanket and disappeared into the dark world of Bram Stoker. He stopped twice to jot down some interesting facts about vampires in his notebook. The bad guys in *All the Vampires Everywhere* were supposedly influenced by Bram Stoker's writing, so maybe, Viktor thought, he could learn a thing or two in the book that might just help him beat the game.

Before he knew it, Dad walked through the front door, which meant he must have been reading for a couple of hours. He sat up, rubbing his eyes, and confirmed that it was well past midnight. It wasn't anything new to see Dad coming home late. He always said he preferred the night shift. "Hey Dad. How are you?"

"Not bad, all things considered. You're up awful late." Dad set his briefcase next to the table in the foyer and stepped into the living room. "Wide awake after a night of partying hard with Damon?"

Viktor shrugged. "Kinda."

He gestured to the book in Viktor's hands with a nod. "Still reading that book, eh?"

"Yeah." Viktor slipped his bookmark between the pages and set the book beside him on the couch. "Did you know Dracula slept in dirt? Like, dirt from his homeland? He had to travel with it and stuff."

"Not exactly believable, is it? Dracula isn't human, which explains the author's need to differentiate him from humans by identifying unusual traits in him. But taking literal dirt naps? If you ask me"—he sighed—"that's a bit much."

"The author did also say Dracula could turn into a wolf, which sounds pretty out there."

"I don't know. It wouldn't be impossible, I guess. There are some rather wild things that exist in nature. So many creatures that scientists discover or rediscover every day. Is it so much of a stretch of our collective imagination to think that a creature could transform their appearance at will? Just look at camouflage in the animal kingdom."

"Yeah, I guess." Viktor shrugged. "I just can't imagine

sleeping in a pile of dirt."

Dad chuckled and gave Viktor's shoulder a squeeze. "Agreed. Give me memory foam any day, son."

As his dad turned to retire upstairs, Viktor opened his book again. But before he could return to reading, thoughts of his conversation with Alys at the Tasty Cow the other day resurfaced. "Hey Dad? Do you think vampires could really exist?"

Dad paused before turning back to face him. "Is there any particular reason you're asking me?"

"No . . ." Viktor blinked at the response, slightly confused at his dad's reaction. "It's just . . . I was talking about the possibility with a friend the other day and I was curious what you thought."

"A friend?"

"Yeah. The new neighbor. Alys."

"Alys." His dad's eyes flicked to the front door, as if he was expecting Alys to bound through it at any moment.

"So do you?"

"Do I what?" Dad tore his gaze away from the door, but something about the way he was acting put Viktor on edge. Why was he being so weird?

"Do you think vampires could actually exist?"

Dad furrowed his brow and went quiet for what felt like an eternity. When Viktor had asked the question, he didn't think it would require so much thought to answer, but apparently, he was wrong. After a while, his dad nodded and said, "I think anything's possible."

As his dad turned back to the stairs, Viktor noticed a small red dot on the front of his dad's shirt. "Hey Dad, you've got a spot of something on your shirt."

He examined the stain for a minute before snapping his fingers, as if he'd just recalled a crucial detail. "Oh. I had a peanut butter and jelly sandwich earlier. I'll make sure to pretreat it before putting it in the laundry. Anyway . . . sleep well, son."

As his dad went up the stairs, Viktor furrowed his brow, rolling over in his mind how odd their conversation had been. Under his breath, he said, "But you hate peanut butter. . . ."

CHAPTER ELEVEN
Does Anybody Really Like Being the Center of Attention?

"You went out with Alys before and didn't tell me?!" Damon's eyes were bulging out of his head. More than anything, Viktor just wanted this conversation to be over.

The truth was, he should have told Damon about hanging out at the Tasty Cow with Alys right after it happened. It wasn't like he hadn't had the opportunity. He could have mentioned it at the party the other night, but for some reason, it made the experience feel even more special to keep it to himself for a while. But now they were walking to school on Monday morning, and telling Damon about it was long overdue. "I know. I should've told you. But it was no big deal. We just hung out, ate food, and talked."

"Did you kiss her after?" Damon cocked an eyebrow before nudging Viktor in the ribs. "Come on. Fess up. I want all the slobbery details."

"What?" Viktor sighed. Sometimes talking to Damon was exhausting. "No. But . . . she did squeeze my hand."

"It's a step in the right direction. We can build on this." Damon was nodding, as if they were planning some kind of heist.

"I just wanna be her friend." *For now*, Viktor thought. He was hoping that brushing off the conversation might help to end it.

"Hey there, Viktor!" Headed down the sidewalk toward them with a bounce in her step was Alys. She was wearing black cargo pants and a T-shirt with an image of Buffy the Vampire Slayer on the front.

At the sight of her, Damon's lips curled up in that gross way they did whenever he saw a girl who he thought was cute. "Whoa. Who is that and why haven't I ever seen her around town before?"

Viktor's stomach ached for some reason that he couldn't identify. Maybe it was the way Damon had noticed Alys. Not that Viktor had called dibs on her or anything. Besides, what kind of jerk called dibs on another person anyway? "That's my new neighbor, Alys. The one we were just talking about five seconds ago."

With his eyes locked on her, Damon asked, "Does 'Alys' rhyme with 'cute'?"

Slowly, and with much confusion, Viktor responded, "No . . ."

As Alys reached them, Damon said under his breath to

Viktor, "Oh, I think it does."

Viktor rolled his eyes. "Damon—"

"Hey there yourself," Damon said to Alys with that same dumb smile on his face. "I hear you just moved in across the street from my friend Viktor here."

"Yeah." She said it like she was just trying to be polite, then moved her attention to Viktor. "I was looking for you earlier. I was going to ask if you wanted to walk to school together."

She'd been looking for him? Nobody ever looked for him, except maybe Damon, but that didn't count.

Viktor offered a casual shrug, trying his best to act like it was totally normal for cute girls to wonder where he was and track him down. "Totally."

Damon cleared his throat—a reminder that he still existed.

Viktor blinked. "Oh. Uh. Alys, this is my friend Damon."

She threw Damon a polite smile. "Nice to meet you."

Damon's weird smile had faded away, but he was still smiling. Viktor thought he just looked confused. He was willing to bet that Damon hadn't been ignored by many people throughout his life—least of all, girls. "Not as nice as it is to meet y—"

She said to Viktor, "You busy Friday? I was wondering if you wanted to come over and watch *Fangs for the Memories* with me."

"Is that the one about a photographer and a vampire who

fall in love even though the vampire doesn't show up on film?" It sounded like a totally eye-rolling, nauseating movie to watch.

But Alys wanted to watch it with *him*.

His heart thumped in a rhythm that reminded him of a song by the Screaming Meemies. He strained, but it took a moment for him to recall the name of the song. *Tardy Doom? Hardy Doom?* Something . . . Then it hit him. "*Doomhearted!*" *Of course. You've only heard it like a million times, Viktor. Get it together, man.*

The words couldn't leave Viktor's lips fast enough. "Sounds great."

"Good. Give me your number." She thrust her phone into his hand with a smile.

He looked from Alys to Damon and back again. Maybe he was dreaming. He'd pinch himself to be certain, but what if it was just a vivid dream? Wouldn't he just feel the pinch anyway and not wake up?

After entering his phone number, he handed her phone back and tried hard to keep his heart inside his chest when her fingers brushed against his.

"Awesome." Her eyes sparkled as she entered the phone into her contacts list. "I'll text ya later."

If he was dreaming, Viktor was determined *not* to pinch himself. Just in case it *would* wake him up. "Cool. See ya."

"See ya!" She was beaming as she skipped ahead of them, toward the front door of the school.

Damon followed Alys with his eyes, which held a mixture of surprise and offense. "Well, that was rude."

"What?"

Damon blinked a few times before responding. "She treated me like I'm invisible."

Damon wasn't mad at Viktor or stuck up or anything. It was just that he was effortlessly great at a lot of things. School was a breeze, friends came easy, parents and teachers loved him, and girls had a habit of fawning over him. So it wasn't like he was being arrogant at the apparent rejection by Alys. It was just that such a thing never happened to him, so Viktor was certain that his best friend was confused at what had just transpired. "Maybe she's in a hurry or something."

"Yeah. Maybe." Damon was still looking off in the direction that Alys had gone. As he turned back to Viktor, he shook his head, as if still confounded by the notion that a girl might not develop an immediate crush on him. "Anyway. I've gotta get to class. We still on for some vampire extermination at my place tonight? Or are you gonna be too busy sucking face with the rude neighbor girl?"

"Dude." Viktor paused, considering the possibility that Alys might want to kiss him. The notion immediately made his stomach tie up into a million knots. He'd never kissed a girl before. "Of course we're on for tonight. Right after school?"

"You know it."

"Cool." Viktor nodded.

Damon turned to walk away, but then, as if a burning thought had made its way to the surface, he turned back again. "Hey, Viktor?"

"Yeah?"

"Be careful, okay? Girls can be weird."

To put his friend's nerves at ease, he said, "Do you know anyone more careful than me?"

After a moment of contemplation that felt out of place for Damon, he shrugged and said, "Point taken. See you at lunch, man."

Viktor stopped by his locker to grab a notebook and pencil before heading to first period. The halls were bustling, but no one bothered him, which he was figuring was a pretty good beginning for a Monday. For any day, really.

When he first entered the classroom, he was a little bummed to find it empty, but just a heartbeat after hanging his messenger bag over the back of his chair, October appeared, coffee in hand. Viktor rummaged through his bag for a moment. "Oh hey, October. I brought something to show you. I thought maybe you'd think it was cool."

After he pulled the book out of his bag and held it up, her eyes winded in undeniable excitement. "Is that a first-edition copy of *Dracula* in mint condition?!"

Viktor was beaming. He knew that if anyone would be over-the-blood-moon excited to see such an old copy of *Dracula*, it would be October. "Near mint. There's some writing in it. Some note to my dad from some guy named Vikas about someone called Elysia."

"Can I see that for a second?" He handed it to her and October flipped to the title page, where the inscription read *For you, my friend, and in ways, for all of Elysia. In Brotherhood, Vikas.* She seemed to read it over and over again, wordlessly obsessing over the writing, as if looking for something that Viktor could not see. The fact that she seemed more obsessed with the dedication than the book itself really threw him for a loop.

"It's kinda a weird inscription, to be honest. My dad doesn't have a brother named Vikas and I'm pretty sure he doesn't know anyone called Elysia."

"Elysia isn't a who. It's not even really a where." She drummed her black nails against the paper for a moment before closing the book and slowly sliding it across the desk toward him. Without meeting his eyes, she sighed and said, "Do yourself a favor, Viktor, and forget you ever heard that word."

Before Viktor had a chance to respond, the bell rang, and all the stragglers rushed into the room to take their seats. October diverted her attention to the class, and all through first period, she seemed to make a point of not glancing Viktor's way the entire time. *Strange*, Viktor thought. *Very strange.*

What was it about that inscription that had unsettled her so much? Why exactly did she think it was so important for

Viktor to forget that he'd ever seen the word *Elysia*? And what was Elysia, if not a person or place?

One thing was for certain. There was no way he was ever going to forget about Elysia, and he was going to do everything he could to find out what it meant.

He drifted through the rest of the school day. Math was boring. PE was obnoxious. Damon made several comments about how distracted Viktor was at lunch, but Viktor couldn't bring himself to explain exactly why. Truth be told, he wasn't sure. He just knew that there was something—something strange and unexplained—linking his English teacher and the inscription inside his father's first-edition copy of *Dracula*.

By the time the last bell of the day rang, Viktor had convinced himself that October must know more about his dad than she'd felt comfortable sharing with him, which absolutely weirded him out. Viktor was just finishing filling his messenger bag with the homework he'd been assigned throughout the day when he realized he'd forgotten his math book in the library. "Be right back, dude."

Damon sighed. "Okay, but hurry up. Every extra minute you spend inside a school after the last bell has rung drains your life three times as fast as usual."

As he approached the library door, he could hear two familiar voices engaged in conversation. Mrs. Conrad and October. Mrs. Conrad said, "Oh, what a gorgeous wedding ring! Is it silver?"

"Oh, no. I'm allergic to silver. Crosses, too, if you ask several of my students."

The sound of their laughter sent a nervous chill up Viktor's spine. Hearing October's words set him on edge. Forget math, he thought. There's no way I'm going in there.

Once he'd rejoined Damon, they exited the school with the energy of two tweens who'd already had enough of the school year . . . even though the school year hadn't yet had enough of them.

Hours later, at Damon's house, Viktor found himself still distracted by the events that took place that morning. Apparently Damon had noticed, because he set his controller down at one point with a sigh and said, "You've been acting bizarro all day, man. What's up?"

"Sorry. I guess I've just been a little out of it."

Damon rolled his eyes. "Yeah, no duh. So what's going on?"

Viktor bit his bottom lip in contemplation, mulling over just what to say. "Do you ever wonder about Mrs. McMillan? Like, where she came from and what she's doing here?"

"You are such a freak. Who thinks about their teachers even a little bit outside of school? Especially their substitute teacher?"

Viktor set his controller on the floor and shrugged. "I mean . . . I dunno. She just kinda popped up outta nowhere and told us she was subbing for Mrs. Harkins, but has anybody heard from Mrs. Harkins? Plus, she's pretty obsessed with vampires."

Damon sighed. "Bro. First off, Mrs. Harkins isn't exactly a social butterfly around town. Second, Mrs. McMillan is so obviously goth. Of course she likes vampires. It's like in the goth handbook or something."

"Okay, fair point about Mrs. Harkins, but it isn't just that October likes vampires. We were talking today and I showed her my dad's first edition of *Dracula* and after she saw the inscription in it, she started acting really weird."

"Weird like how?"

"I don't know. Just weird." Viktor glanced over at his messenger bag. The flap at the top was open, revealing his dad's copy of *Dracula*. "Hey, have you ever heard of something called Elysia?"

Damon took a swig of Mountain Dew before responding. "What's that? Like some kind of plant or something?"

The save screen kept playing its animation over and over again, as if the game were waiting for the boys to finish their conversation and get back to hacking vampires to bloody chunks. Viktor watched it for a while before speaking again. It was hard to say the things he'd been thinking, but if he could say them to anyone, it was Damon. "I don't know exactly what it is, but the guy who wrote in my dad's book mentioned it and it wigged October out. What if it's some kind of secret code for people who are into vampires or something? What if I wasn't ever supposed to know about it because I'm not in whatever secret club October is in? And what if my dad's in that same club?"

Damon sat up suddenly, snapping his fingers. "Roman heaven."

Clearly, his best friend had gone insane. "Excuse me?"

"Weren't the Elysian fields like Roman heaven or Greek heaven or some kinda afterlife thing?"

Viktor tried linking the words he'd read scribbled in the cover of his dad's book with the bits and pieces of mythology that Damon had just brought up, but he couldn't see a link between them. "Can you focus please?"

"You asked me a question!" Damon looked him over and when Viktor offered no response, he said, "Hey . . . seriously, though. Are you okay?"

"Yeah." He stretched, even though he didn't really feel like stretching. "Just tired, I guess. I'm gonna head home."

When he finally stepped outside, Viktor noted how dark it had gotten in the hours they'd been playing *All the Vampires Everywhere* and moved down the sidewalk, toward the end of town he called home. It was a short walk, but an uneventful one—something Viktor considered to be a small blessing. As he turned to go inside his house, he glanced up to Alys's bedroom window. Viktor's life was changing—maybe in enormous ways—and he was feeling surprised, anxious, and delighted. A far cry from just feeling anxious.

Across the street and down a block, Viktor noticed his dad, who was dressed in ratty sneakers, calf-length socks, running shorts that looked like he'd bought them in the 1980s, and a T-shirt that read "Dad jokes? I think you mean rad jokes!"

Just in front of him was a blond woman wearing running gear that looked much better put together than his dad's. They kept in pace together as they ran, and Viktor wondered who she was. A new friend maybe? A coworker?

"Dad! Hey, Dad!" He waved an arm to get his dad's attention, but his dad must not have heard or seen him. With a shrug, Viktor walked inside his house and followed the scent of fresh bread to the kitchen, where his mother was kneading dough.

On the table, beside his school copy of *Dracula*, was a basket of fresh baked cookies. Grabbing one, he took a bite and said, "Hey, Mom. Since when does Dad go jogging?"

With an absent-minded tone, she said, "Jogging?"

"Yeah. I just saw him running down the street. And don't most people go running in the morning? It's dark out."

His mom paused her kneading for a moment before flipping the dough on its other side and continuing to work it. "I'm sure it wasn't your father you saw, Viktor."

"No, I'm positive it was him. He was wearing those horrible shorts. You know. The ones he wears with those stupid tube socks with the stripes?"

Mom was quiet for a second before responding. "Oh. Well, he has been trying to take care of his health better. Maybe he's just experimenting with a new form of cardio."

Viktor wrinkled his nose. He guessed that what his mom was saying made sense. Except for the fact that he'd never seen his dad exercise one day in his entire life. His dad had just always been naturally fit. So why he'd take up jogging out of the blue was beyond Viktor. But then . . . adults were weird. "I guess. But that doesn't explain the woman who was running with him."

Clucking her tongue, she wiped her hands clean with a towel and reached for a small box that had been sitting on the counter behind her. "I almost forgot. You got a package in the mail today. I think it's from your Aunt Carmilla."

"What is it?"

His mom chuckled and handed him the box. "I don't know, silly. You have to open it."

The package was wrapped in the same waxy brown paper that all of Aunt Carmilla's packages came wrapped in. This one had words stamped on it in some language Viktor couldn't understand, which meant that she'd sent it from some other country. It didn't surprise him. Aunt Carmilla was always on the move. She'd once told him that she kept an apartment so she had somewhere to store all her books. At the time he'd thought it was a joke. But then he'd visited her home and almost got lost in the stacks and stacks of books. Aunt Carmilla loved to read. Viktor was willing to bet Mrs. Conrad would love her.

"Is she still coming for a visit next month?" Viktor tugged at the seams of the wrapping paper until the paper came free.

"I'm not sure. Something came up, so she may come sooner. Maybe as soon as next week." She returned to working her dough. Then, as she was greasing a bread pan, she said, "Hmm. We should get the guest room ready, just in case."

"Is Aunt Laura coming too this time?"

"As far as I know, yes."

Aunt Carmilla was pretty awesome, but her wife, Aunt Laura, was downright cool. She was younger than Carmilla and always made time to play games with Hannah and sneak out at night with Viktor so they could go on late-night drives, drink way too much caffeine, and blare the radio nice and loud while they sang along to whatever music was playing—usually off-key. He wasn't sure if Mom, Dad, and Carmilla had any idea about their late-night adventures, but that just made it cooler. Aunt Laura couldn't always make it for a visit, but when she could, it was unforgettable.

He flipped the box over and elation filled him. "I can't believe she did it! Aunt Carmilla sent me the demo for *All the Zombies Everywhere (Except for North Dakota)*! It doesn't even come out for another six months! She said she could get one. This is unreal. I have to text Damon."

His mom smiled. "Of course she got it for you. Carmilla has some very important contacts, including royalty. You don't think she might know someone in the video game industry?"

"Mom, kings and queens are one thing. These are *game*

devs . . ." The front door opened, and Viktor heard his dad take off his shoes and sigh. With his eyes practically devouring the description on the back of the game he was holding, he called out, "Hey, Dad. Guess what Aunt Carmilla—"

His words failed him when his dad entered the kitchen.

Because something was wrong. His stomach did somersaults as he looked at his dad. The room started to spin. He felt lightheaded, and with good reason. There was something on Dad's lips. And that something was deep red in color.

Blood. Dad had blood on his face. On his . . . mouth.

"What did my big sister do now?" His dad met his eyes then and his expression grew from bemusement to absolute confusion and concern. "Is something wrong, Viktor?"

A small drip of crimson drew a line from the corner of his dad's mouth to the tip of his chin.

"Umm . . ." Viktor's jaw began to tremble. He was growing ever more certain that he was going pass ou—

Viktor stirred. It took him a moment to realize that he was lying on the kitchen floor, a folded towel under his head. His mom brushed his hair back from his forehead, a worried look on her face. "Viktor? Are you all right? You fainted."

Viktor sat up with care. "Yeah. I just . . ."

His mom gasped as she turned to face Dad. "Oh dear, did you split your lip again?"

Viktor looked at his father. He had never seen his dad

bleed so much before—especially from something as simple as a split lip. What's more, the blood didn't seem to be coming from his dad's lip. It was more like it was coming from inside his mouth.

"Oh. I . . ." His dad's eyes went wide, and a silent conversation seemed to pass between him and Mom. "Yes. Yes, I split my lip again. I need to start using ChapStick. The air's been so dry. I'll just go get cleaned up."

Dad bent to ruffle Viktor's hair and he passed by wearing a calm smile on his face once more. But all Viktor could focus on was the nervous look in his parents' eyes, the blood on his father's chin . . .

. . . and the copy of *Dracula* that was sitting on the kitchen table.

CHAPTER TWELVE
Debriefing

"Does he have a regular routine? Any weaknesses you can determine?" The woman's tone was bordering on the edges of impatient.

The girl finished chewing a bite of green beans as she returned her fork to her dinner plate. The sky outside was turning a goldish pink hue. She wiped the corners of her mouth with her napkin before setting it on the table. "Not that I know of . . . yet. But I'll find out everything we need to know. I just need more time."

The woman's mouth pursed in something that resembled anger but wasn't quite that. "We should strike fast and hard while we know where he's located."

The girl shook her head in exasperation. She was good at her job. Excellent, even. Or she had been until the last one. But didn't everyone deserve a little slack? "If we take our time, we can do this right. We've been on his trail for so long. With just a little patience and some time, we can end him and this whole thing is over."

"Will he trust you?" The man spoke for the first time since they sat down at the table.

"I'll make sure of it," the girl said with certainty.

The woman took a sip of water and returned her glass to the table. "If he learns of our plans—"

The girl snapped her eyes to the woman. "Then you can both blame me forever and punish me however you wish."

"She won't fail. Not this time." The man met her gaze and raised one sharp eyebrow. She thought it might have been a threat but couldn't be sure. "Will you, Alys?"

Alys swallowed hard, remembering a time not so long ago when she'd almost screwed things up bad enough to undo a mission that they'd committed to for two entire years. "Not this time, Father. Not again. Never again."

Her father's voice was gruff . . . threatening, even, as his eyes met hers. "Make sure of it. Make no mistake. We're not leaving here until he is dead."

The task stretched out before Alys like a desert that felt impossible to cross. But she had to cross it. And to do that, she had to get as close to Viktor Valentine as she was able to.

CHAPTER THIRTEEN
A Question of Trust

The next morning, Viktor still couldn't get the image of his dad's blood-covered mouth and the silent conversation between his parents out of the forefront of his mind. So much so that he'd risen an hour earlier than usual, grabbed a quick shower, and hurried off to school without breakfast or so much as a text to Damon. Mrs. Conrad had greeted him with a confused smile. "Good morning, Viktor. You're here earlier than normal."

"Yeah. I just . . ." He shifted his feet a little. He wasn't sure why he was feeling so nervous talking to Mrs. Conrad about finding some books. She was a librarian, after all. It was kinda their thing. "Do you have any more books about vampires?"

"*Dracula* piqued your interest, eh?"

"Um, something like that," he said, nodding,

"Well, I have more books on vampires than you could ever need. The kids in this town love their vampire stories. What are you looking for? Horror? Action? Humor? Romance?"

"More like . . ." His heart beat three times before the last word left his lips. "History."

Mrs. Conrad tapped the tip of her forefinger against her lips, deep in thought. He imagined that if he could take a stroll inside her brain, it would look much like the library they were standing in. "Hmm . . . if it's cultural history you're looking for—"

"Anything, I guess." He shrugged. "To be honest, I'm not sure what I'm looking for."

"Okay." The look in her eyes suggested that he'd just uttered the magic words. "In that case, I'll get you a little bit of everything, and if none of those pan out, I'll look for more. Sound good? I'll leave a pile at the front desk. You can pick them up after school."

"Thanks, Mrs. Conrad."

That afternoon, Viktor was back home in his bedroom, poring over the books that Mrs. Conrad had lent him. She hadn't limited him to four books, as dictated by library policy, but instead sent him with an armload of thirteen—a wide variety of genres and context. From a scary vampire neighbor in a small Maine town to a whiny vampire in New Orleans who wore more ruffles on his shirt than should be legal; from a German pointy-eared weirdo who'd appeared in some silent movie a million years ago to a half-human, half-vampire guy from a small town not so different from the one that Viktor called home.

It was a lot of information to digest, and, if Viktor was being honest with himself, he wasn't certain what he was looking for in any of the books. So his dad had come home with blood on his lips. So what? So his mom had been soaking a blood-drenched shirt in the sink the other day. What was the big deal? So the air between him and his parents had been kinda strange in the past few weeks. It didn't mean he was dealing with anything remotely vampiric. Besides, everybody knew that vampires weren't real.

Didn't they?

Viktor wasn't so sure anymore. It was an awful lot of blood for a split lip—a split that Viktor couldn't see after his dad had cleaned up. And his dad had been acting strange in recent weeks—running out in the middle of the night, offering up pretty pathetic explanations about where he was going or why he and Mom held long, whispered conversations after he returned. Conversations that ended the moment that Viktor entered the room. It was clear that something was up. But vampires?

Maybe he'd been reading *Dracula* a bit too much without reminding himself that it was a work of pure fiction.

Apart from all the virtual vampire killing, the house was quiet. Mom was helping Hannah sell cookies for her

Sprinkles troop. Dad was down the street fixing their neighbor's lawn mower. And Damon and Viktor had just finished level three of *All the Vampires Everywhere*. The plan was to beat this game before they even touched the demo of *All the Zombies Everywhere (Except for North Dakota)*, but at the rate Viktor kept dying, it was never going to happen. Damon didn't complain, though. Even if it was pretty apparent that Viktor was the sole reason why they'd yet to beat the game in over a month of playing. It was yet another example of Damon being the perfect person to talk to about his dad: he was easygoing and understanding, and he had Viktor's back.

After taking a swig of Mountain Dew to moisten his dry mouth, Viktor said, "Do you believe in monsters?"

Emitting a wistful sigh, Damon replied, "I believe in beating them so we can move on to the next level, yeah."

"Not those monsters."

Damon set the bag of Doritos he'd been holding on the floor and said, "What do you mean? Like politicians being jerks? Sure."

"Not that. I mean, like, real monsters." Viktor swallowed hard, considering the possibility. "Really real."

"Most politicians are pretty fake, but they do exist." Damon rolled his eyes.

"No, I mean . . . actual monsters. As in ghosts and werewolves and . . ." As Damon reached for his controller, Viktor finished his sentence. ". . . vampires?"

Damon paused and sat back, looking his best friend in the eye. "Are you being weird right now, or is this a serious discussion topic?"

"I'm serious." He knew he sounded like he'd been watching too many documentaries about monsters, cryptids, and things that went bump in the night. But if he could spout wild ideas to anyone and count on not being judged, it was Damon.

"Is this the conversation that's going to explain the mountains of books about vampires in your room? I mean, it's one thing to have a hobby, dude, but the vampire thing is kinda becoming an obsession for you."

"I'm not obsessed, I just . . . have a healthy curiosity." He sighed, contemplating his next words. "Have you ever thought that maybe stuff like that could exist?"

Damon shrugged. "I guess anything's possible. Why?"

"Because I think I saw one." The memory of seeing his dad running behind that woman (or was it *after* her?) filled his mind, followed by the image of blood on his dad's mouth. "Maybe. I dunno."

Damon's eyes went wide. "No way, for real? Details, man! Fork 'em over!"

Viktor thought about just how to phrase that he thought there might be a possibility that his dad wasn't just a member of the PTA, but also a blood-drinking monster. "You won't laugh?"

"Dude, you've seen me in those pink dragon pajamas my

aunt made for me last Christmas. Trust me . . . there's no way I'm gonna laugh at you." The look on his face told Viktor he meant business. But that didn't make this any easier.

"You know me, Damon. I'm not someone who sees stuff where there's nothing to see, right?"

"Right."

With a deep breath, Viktor said, "I think . . . I know it sounds weird, but I think something's up with my dad."

Damon raised an eyebrow. "Something . . . like maybe he's not human?"

"Yeah. I know it sounds nuts, but I . . . I think he could be a vampire. Like a real one." Viktor's chest felt tight. Saying it out loud, he didn't just wonder if he was weird, he knew he was. What kind of person believed in vampires, let alone suspected their dad might be one, despite the fact that he'd not seen any other so-called evidence in his twelve years on Earth?

Damon seemed to mull it over for a moment.

At last, Damon shrugged. "Eh, I've heard weirder things."

"Really?" Relief washed over Viktor. "Like what?"

"Oh, like that rumor that was floating around about vampires creating PlayStation. Can you imagine? If vampires created any kind of system, it'd be Xbox, for sure." Chuckling, he grabbed a handful of Doritos and shoved them in his mouth, chewing.

"I'm serious. Something weird is going on."

"And you're jumping straight to vampires?" There it was.

Damon's questioning eyebrow. To tell the truth, sometimes Viktor hated seeing it. Damon said, "You know what we need to do, right?"

"What?"

"A recon mission. You bring the caffeine. I'll bring my uncle's binoculars."

Viktor blinked. "No joke?"

Damon shrugged. "Bro, if you say something's off, then something is off. The only way to find out just how off is to do a close observation and thorough investigation. And maybe Twinkies. Bring those too."

Viktor's chest loosened up and he could breathe again. "Thanks, man."

"For what? Believing you? That's what friends do, man." After taking a swig of Mountain Dew, he said, "When do you wanna dive in?"

"Dive in?"

"Yeah. Our reconnaissance mission. I'm thinking of calling it Operation: Loch Ness."

Viktor blinked again. "How does this have anything to do with the Loch Ness Monster?"

"Well, nobody has any idea if she's real either, but people keep looking anyway."

"She?"

Damon shrugged and picked up his controller, ready to face the vampire housewife in level four. "Just a theory I have."

Despite the sick, worried feeling in his stomach, Viktor managed a smile. He picked up his controller too and braced himself for all of the bloodshed coming their way in the next level. "Well, I guess Operation: Loch Ness starts tonight after dark. If that's cool with you."

"Doing a recon mission in real life and maybe proving monsters are real?" Damon grinned. "What could be cooler than that?"

CHAPTER FOURTEEN
Operation: Loch Ness

The table on Viktor's balcony was littered with about a dozen empty soda cans, three empty bags that had contained a variety of chips, and about a million candy wrappers if Viktor's count was right. Damon was holding his uncle's binoculars. Those were the only major supplies they'd brought along for their reconnaissance . . . which kinda seemed a little sad to Viktor. He didn't know what he'd been picturing. Ski masks? Cups of coffee? Night-vision goggles? He hated coffee and wouldn't even know where to buy a pair of night-vision goggles, though he suspected you could find some online. You could find pretty much anything online—both good things and pretty friggin' terrible things.

Just about the only thing they had easy access to were ski masks, but on second thought, that seemed more like something a bank robber would wear and less like something a superspy or whatever would wear. In the end, they'd settled for junk food and binoculars.

Not to mention four hours of disappointment.

Viktor sat back in his seat with an impatient groan. "See anything?"

With a grumpy tone, Damon said, "Bro, we're facing the same direction. Do *you* see anything?"

"*You* have the binoculars. *I'm* not looking through them. Which you would *see* if you turned your head to the left!" Viktor knew he had snapped and immediately felt sorry. It was okay though. They were both exhausted and disappointed that the evening hadn't taught them any more than they knew when they'd turned off the Xbox earlier. "I'm sorry. I'm just frustrated. Doesn't mean I should take it out on you."

"Don't worry about it. I'm not having the easiest time at home, so I'm sorry if I'm not the greatest company."

"Your mom's boyfriend?"

"Ugh. Yes." Damon threw his head back, dramatically rolling his eyes. "It's not like he's not a nice guy or anything, but every time he's around I wish a T. rex would appear out of nowhere and chew him to death, y'know?"

"Who hasn't felt that way about someone, really?"

Damon's eyes were focused on his feet, but Viktor was willing to bet just about anything that his attention was focused on all the changes going on in Damon's family right now. He was quiet for a long time before speaking again, and when he did, his voice was hushed. "Things were okay, y'know? Not great, but before my dad died, things were all right. Then that stupid accident took him away and three years later, my life is unrecognizable. I'm just . . . tired of change."

Viktor gave him a slap on the back. "Well, I'm never changing. So, you can count on that."

"You'd better not. I'm not sure how much more I can take." Damon's sigh was loud, heavy, and showed just how frustrated he was. On top of everything, it seemed Operation: Loch Ness was a bust. "Maybe your dad doesn't feel like going for a jog tonight."

Viktor geared up for the thing he was about to share with his friend—the thing he'd shoved hard to the back of his mind because he was afraid to think about it. "I told you. That wasn't the only weird thing. I overheard him and Mom talking about someone the other night—the night after the first day of school—and I swear I heard my dad say, 'If I have to kill him myself, I will.'"

Damon's eyes went wide. "Dude! You didn't tell me that!"

"Maybe I heard wrong. My dad is the most chill person on the planet." He hoped he was wrong. More than anything. "Anyway, add that to the way he's been acting lately and . . . well . . . *something's* gotta be up with him for sure. I mean, what else could it be?"

After some brief consideration, Damon sighed. "We may

have to consider the less-fun possibility that your dad is just a boring old human and not an undead creature of the night."

Viktor was conflicted. On one hand, the idea of his dad being an actual real-life vampire terrified him to his core. On the other, it would be pretty cool to have a dad who could turn into a bat at will. "Whatever it is, I just want to understand."

Damon shrugged. "Maybe he's a serial killer."

"Damon! My dad's not a serial killer."

There it was again. Damon's raised eyebrow. "Is that any less realistic than him being a vampire?"

Sighing, Viktor said, "I guess we should clean up and go back inside. You staying over?"

"Nah. My mom is cracking down on me staying out on school nights, so . . ."

"Gross."

"Tell me about it." Damon blinked, as if waking from a dream. Or a nightmare. A strict-curfew kind of nightmare. "Anyway, sorry Operation: Loch Ness didn't pan out. Maybe we can try again tomorrow night."

"Yeah, maybe."

"Hey. It'll be okay. You know that, right?" Damon met Viktor's eyes. Viktor wished more than anything that he could agree with his friend, but things felt about as far away from okay as they could get. As if understanding Viktor's thoughts, Damon nodded and said, "Anyway, I've gotta go. See ya, man."

"See ya."

As Viktor began picking up the discarded wrappers and empty cans, he thought about the things he'd seen and wondered once again if maybe he'd just been imagining things that weren't true. Maybe his dad *had* been jogging. Maybe his lip really had split. After twelve years, didn't he owe his dad the benefit of a doubt?

Besides, vampires weren't real.

Were they?

October's words echoed in the back of his mind. *"I'm allergic to silver. Crosses, too . . ."*

Movement on the street below caught his attention and, after a heartbeat, he looked at the person making his way up the street with determined steps. Viktor squinted to be certain, and what he saw sent a wave of concern over the very core of his being. It was Dad. Leaving the house at two in the morning. He was holding something in his hand, but Viktor couldn't make out what it was. His dad kept looking over his shoulder every few yards, as if he was worried someone might be following him. Viktor wondered who he worried that might be. His mom? Him?

Viktor kept his eyes on his dad for another block. His pace had picked up, matching the rhythm of Viktor's heartbeat. Viktor's chest tightened until it felt like a giant snake was about to have him for dinner. "I need to follow him," he mumbled.

With a lump in his throat, he snuck downstairs and out

the front door. The house was dark and still. Mom and Hannah were sleeping.

The night air felt cool on Viktor's skin as he walked at a brisk pace. He kept his distance from his dad up ahead, moving between houses and trees, keeping to the shadows so that he wouldn't be seen. His dad had stopped looking over his shoulder, which made it easier for Viktor to tail him. Viktor wondered how far he was going to walk, but he had his answer fifteen minutes later when they reached the opposite end of town, where the mausoleum of Nowhere's founder, Travion Jett, stood.

It was a small building and nowhere near a cemetery—in fact, the nearest cemetery was two towns over. The stone was aged and darkened by time and the elements. Ornate arches lined the roof and two winged statues stood sentinel on either side of the patinaed copper door. They weren't angels. Viktor wasn't quite sure what they were supposed to be. Their wings looked more like bat wings, and their icy stares were turned somewhat inward so that if you stood in front of the door, it looked as if they were staring right at you in the most unnerving way. Viktor knew that because Damon had dared him to knock on the door last year at Halloween.

It was a stupid dare that every kid in Nowhere was subjected to at some point in their life. The rumor was that if you stood between the statues in front of Travion Jett's mausoleum on Halloween night and knocked thirteen times, he would appear. It would be impressive enough, but the urban legend added the intriguing twist that Travion Jett was a vampire—something that Viktor had always thought was stupid. After all, vampires weren't real.

Were they?

He wondered if maybe the town myth had seeped into his brain and that's why he wondered if his dad might be a vampire. When you grow up hearing the same story every Halloween, it kinda sticks with you. Maybe this all was a misunderstanding. Maybe Viktor was just getting lost in his imagination. *After all*, he thought, *it wouldn't be the first time.*

But standing in front of the mausoleum now was a man that Viktor had never seen before. He was dressed in a dark crimson suit, black shirt and matching shoes, and a tie matching the suit, which reminded Viktor of the line of blood dripping down from the corner of his dad's mouth. His dad was talking to the man, but Viktor couldn't hear what was being said until he snuck behind a nearby hedge. With quiet care, he found a thin spot in the hedge, held his breath, and watched.

"I told you, Your Excellency, I haven't an inkling what he's doing here." The man's voice was smooth—as silky as his tie. His tone suggested that he wasn't a huge fan of Nowhere. He wasn't the first to feel that way. "Of all places."

"Dying soon, if I have my way." His dad's face looked gaunt in the moonlight. Sadness haunted his eyes. Viktor bit his bottom lip, recalling the conversation he'd overheard between his parents. It couldn't be him his dad was talking about. His parents loved him.

Didn't they?

The man in the crimson suit paused, tilting his head some, as if deep in thought. "Does your son know about your . . . affliction? Does he know about Elysia?"

Elysia. Viktor stretched his memory to find the familiar word. He found it scribbled in his dad's first-edition copy of Dracula. But what did it mean?

"No. It would just complicate things further."

Another pause. Then the man said, "Your Excellency, why have you called me here? How may I be of assistance?"

Your excellency? Wasn't that something reserved for royalty? Was that the big secret? Was Dad a king or lord or something and not a vampire at all? And if so, did that make Viktor a prince? More importantly, did princes get early access to video games if they wanted? Because that would make wearing some dumb crown around worth it.

Dad turned his head toward the hedge that Viktor was hiding behind. Viktor's heart shot into his throat, threatening to choke him. His dad said, "Did you hear something?"

"Nothing but the paranoid tone in your voice."

"Watch your words, Ruthven." Dad shot the guy a look that said he meant business.

Ruthven? What kind of name was Ruthven?

"Apologies, Your Excellency." The man in the suit lowered

his gaze. "Is the countess aware of the situation at hand?"

"No. Which is one of the reasons we're meeting here. I can't have her know everything. Not yet. It would break her heart. She knows enough. The rest will come after his demise."

"My, you are bursting with secrets, aren't you?" The hint of a bemused smile danced across the man's lips. "If the countess doesn't know about whatever it is that you have planned, it must be serious. How may I assist you?"

Dad held up a piece of rolled up parchment, tied closed with a ribbon the same color as the Ruthven guy's suit. As he handed it over, he said, "I need you to take this to Lilith."

Ruthven's fingers curled around the paper, as if he were hesitant to touch it. "A bold move. Are you certain?"

"Certain?" Dad's eyes were glistening with the threat of tears. "No. I'm desperate."

Ruthven nodded and slid the parchment into an inside pocket of his suit. When he spoke again, his tone was no longer the tone of a servant to royalty, but that of a good friend who was worried. "I don't mean to intrude on your plans, but I could make this so much easier and dispatch him while I'm here. It would be quick, painless, and over with. There's no need to involve her."

Dad shook his head. "No, this is a letter long overdue. And an act that I've avoided doing for fear of the pain of the loss of him."

"I understand."

"Thank you, Ruthven. Your assistance is appreciated in this manner." Viktor had never heard his dad speak with such a formal tone. It was weird. Even weirder to think that this was the same guy who tormented his family with dad jokes and puns.

"I am at eternally your disposal, Your Excellency." Ruthven paused again and then raised a sharp eyebrow. "Are you certain you won't change your mind about having him killed?"

"Certain enough." The dam broke, and tears fell from his eyes. "I'll mourn him, but what other choice do I have?"

There was only one male person in Viktor's dad's life that he would cry about losing, and that was his son.

Viktor felt the panic rise in his chest once again . . . but this time it came with a side of terror.

CHAPTER FIFTEEN
How Big Do Snakes Get, Anyway?

The lone walk to school the next morning was brutal for Viktor—both because he was exhausted after staying up so late the night before, and that whole maybe-his-dad-wanted-to-kill-him-for-some-unforeseen-reason thing. It all felt like some weird, random nightmare, but then Viktor would recall small details, like the man named Ruthven's raised eyebrow and the tears in his dad's eyes, and the reality of it would come flooding in with a force so strong it made Viktor's chest ache. What was he going to do? His dad apparently wasn't a vampire but did want him dead. He'd considered calling the police, but until he knew what was going on and why, he didn't want to risk tearing his family apart. Plus, what would he say?

He kept thinking about his mom and Hannah and how

they would react when they found out about Dad and what he was planning. The looks on their faces—filled with so much anger and pain—sent a spiderweb crack straight through the center of his heart. How could his dad want him dead? It made no sense. Well . . . it made more sense than that ridiculous theory that his dad might be a vampire, anyway.

"Good morning, Viktor. You okay?" October was sitting at her desk, looking somewhat concerned. After a quick glance at the wall clock, she said, "Anxious to get started today?"

Viktor shook his thoughts away. "I . . . I'm sorry. I guess I'm just . . . a bit distracted this morning."

"Something on your mind?"

Viktor shook his head. "It's nothing. Really."

She didn't look convinced. "How goes the *Dracula* paper?"

"It's coming along, I guess. I think I got a little sucked into the lore. It kinda messed with my head for a while." *That was one way to put it*, he thought.

"When I was your age, I was pretty obsessed with vampire lore. But that obsession led me to some interesting places."

"Like where?"

She shrugged. "Well, because of it, I made some of the best friends I ever had."

Must be nice, he thought. He'd only ever really had the one friend in Damon. Well, until Alys, he supposed.

She paused with her gaze fixed on him for what felt like a

long time, as if she was debating how much to tell him about her younger self. "Y'know, Viktor, if you want to talk about anything, I happen to be a great listener—or at least that's what I've been told."

He chewed his bottom lip for a moment in contemplation. "Can I ask you something? Just between us?"

"Of course." Her smile was warm and natural. It reminded Viktor of his mom.

He thought about asking her more about Elysia, but thought better of it. "How do you know if, like, you're doing the right thing?"

"In what situation?"

"Any situation, I guess." Especially a situation that involved a person's dad, unexplained blood, and a covert meeting with a strange man in a red suit. "But, I mean, let's say you learned that somebody you cared about was planning to do something awful, and you know you need to tell someone, but if you tell that certain someone you need to tell, it will hurt the person you cared about. Hypothetically, I mean. How do you decide whether to tell or not?"

"Hmm. That one's a thinker. I've got to hand it to you, Viktor. When you open up, you *really* open up." She chuckled at first but quickly regained her composure. "May I ask what the hypothetical awful thing is?"

"I'd rather not say." For one thing, he didn't want his dad to go to prison. For another, he was pretty sure she'd think he was weird and just imagining things. The same thing he thought about himself when he thought his dad might be a vampire.

She pursed her lips for a moment as she mulled over his question. "Well . . . if someone I cared for were, let's say, planning to hurt me, the first thing I'd do is approach them directly, tell them that I know what they're planning, and ask them why."

Viktor's throat felt dry. "How am I supposed to do that? I'm . . . well, I'm kinda scared, to be honest."

She tilted her head as she looked at him. "Viktor, what's going on? I want to help you if I can, but for me to do that, I need to know what's happening."

"No offense, October, but you're a teacher. If I tell you about something bad that happened, you're legally obligated to tell someone, and I just can't handle that right now."

Her feelings looked a little hurt, but she made it clear she'd heard him when she said, "Got it. You do know that I'm just trying to help protect you, right? I may be an authority figure, but that doesn't mean I don't care about you."

"I know."

"Can I offer you some advice, at least?" After he nodded, she said, "Fear is a powerful thing, but you can either let it push you back . . . or you can use it to propel you forward."

Viktor bit the inside of his cheek for a moment before speaking. "Hey, October . . . do you think that vampires could maybe actually exist?"

"I believe anything is possible." She tilted her head some,

eyeing him with curiosity. "Why do you ask?"

"Just . . . thinking out loud, I guess. What would you do if you came across one?"

She shrugged. "Personally? I'd make friends with him. But that's just me."

Viktor couldn't imagine anything more dangerous. "You'd befriend a monster?"

"Billionaires are monsters, Viktor. Politicians are monsters. Vampires are just people. Like you and me, only with a very particular diet and an allergy to garlic and sunlight." As if she suddenly felt the need to busy herself, she began organizing the papers on her desk into two distinct piles. "Having fangs doesn't automatically make them evil."

"But . . . they're not real. Are they?"

October shrugged. "I guess that depends on your definition of the word *real*."

Her words echoed in his mind all through English, math, and PE. By the time he entered the cafeteria for lunch, he had a pretty good idea what he was going to do about the fear he felt. He was going to use it to find out what was going on with his dad.

Moments later, he and Damon were seated close to the windows. Damon had folded his arms on the table and was resting his chin on them, looking up at his friend like he'd lost his mind. "You couldn't bring this up during PE?"

"When was I supposed to bring it up exactly? Between push-ups?"

"You think your dad is in the mob? Dude, that sounds crazy."

Viktor tried to wrap his head around Damon's sense of logic but was coming up empty. It shouldn't have surprised him. Damon was the sole inhabitant on Planet Damon. "Wait a minute. You were willing to consider that my dad might be a vampire, but you can't imagine him being in the mob?"

Damon said, "I'm just sayin'. It sounds like something out of a movie."

"And vampires don't?"

"Hey man." Damon shrugged with the casual air of someone who didn't have a dad that was trying to kill him. "We don't know how big snakes get."

Viktor felt like his head might just actually explode. "What are you talking about?! What do snakes have to do with this subject?!"

"Think about it. Scientists don't know how large snakes can get. They have theories, but no one *really* knows. So, if we don't know that one thing about our own planet, who's to say that vampires don't exist?"

Viktor sat there, staring at his best friend in disbelief. After a moment, he said, "I hate that that makes sense to me."

"All that matters is that it *does* make sense."

The cafeteria was full of people moving this way and that, carrying on loud conversations just so they could be sure they'd been heard. Viktor was grateful for that. After all, the last thing he wanted was for anyone else to overhear what they were discussing.

Which was snakes, apparently.

Raking his hair back from his face, Viktor sighed in frustration. "Well, if he's not a mobster, why would he talk to that Ruthven guy about killing me?"

Damon shrugged. "Maybe he wasn't talking about you."

"Dude, he said . . ." Viktor strained to recall the exact words his dad had used but couldn't recall him saying "I want Viktor dead" exactly. "Okay, he may not have said my name, but he *was* talking about having some guy killed and he seemed upset at the idea. So . . ."

"So? Wouldn't you be upset about the idea of anybody getting killed?" Damon raised his eyebrow and looked at Viktor in a way that said he knew he was making perfect sense—maybe not snake-size sense, but sense. The trouble was, Viktor knew it too.

"Well, yeah. But . . ." It didn't sound like something his dad would do, and once again he wondered if he'd just imagined the whole thing. Why was he targeting his dad? Labeling him a vampire? A mobster? He mulled over the evidence he'd witnessed before speaking once again. "I told you about that conversation I overheard between my mom and dad."

"And if you did hear them right, during that convo, did they discuss having *you* killed? Like by name?"

Viktor thought about it and, blinking, said, "Well . . . no."

With a sigh, Damon said, "Look, I believe you. I do. I just think maybe your dad doesn't have a contract out on you. Is it so hard to believe that this whole thing may be just a misunderstanding?"

It was possible that Damon was right, but even though it would alleviate a million pounds of stress, Viktor didn't want to admit it. He needed answers, reasons for the things he had witnessed. After hearing his parents and then his dad discussing it with that strange man in a red suit who Viktor had never seen or heard of before, how could he entertain the very idea that maybe he was wrong, and maybe the whole thing was just a weird series of misunderstandings? "But if it's not me he wants killed, then who could it be?"

"There's one way to find out." Damon flashed him a look that he knew well. It was the look of "dude, it is so obvious." He'd seen it many times before.

Viktor groaned. "Please tell me you're not going to suggest Operation: Loch Ness part two."

"Of course not." His tone suggested that he'd never suggest such a thing, but Viktor knew Damon better than Damon knew himself. "We're just gonna ask him."

"What? No."

Sitting back in his seat with a look of surprise, Damon said, "No?"

Viktor set his jaw with determination. The time for questions was over. Now it was time for answers. "I'm going to ask him. Just me. But I've gotta wait till the time is right. I have to get him alone."

From the moment he left school that afternoon, Viktor tried hard not to think about his dad and focused instead on his movie night with Alys. He kept glancing at his phone, waiting for Alys to text him, wondering if she ever would. He was about to give up hope when his phone buzzed with her text at last. Ready for movie time?

He typed out a response, deleted it, typed out another one, and deleted that as well. He finally settled on Yeah!!! but immediately regretted the multiple exclamation points.

There was a pause on Alys's end and Viktor was convinced that his punctuation choice had ruined everything. But then she texted: I've got buttery popcorn and bottles of soda waiting. Come over!!!

A sigh of relief escaped his lungs upon seeing her use of exclamation points. Maybe he hadn't blown it after all. On my way!

He tried not to hurry out the door and across the street, but the fact was, he was excited. A woman—Alys's mom, maybe—was pulling out of their driveway by the time he got to Alys's house. When he reached her door, he rang the bell and waited just a single heartbeat before Alys opened the door wearing a broad smile.

"Hey there. Come on in." She opened the door wide, and once Viktor had entered the house, she gestured to a man dressed in an array of earth tones, right down to his tweed vest. The only thing he wore that wasn't a color that would blend into the background with ease was his crisp white shirt—the sleeves of which were rolled up to his elbows, as if he had hard work ahead of him. "This is my dad."

Her dad smiled and extended a hand. When Viktor shook his hand, he noticed that her dad's skin was just as warm as the colors he wore. "Nice to meet you, Viktor. You can call me Abraham."

"Nice to meet you too, sir. Abraham."

"Alys has told me quite a bit about you. It's good to meet you in person at last."

Viktor wondered how much she could tell her dad about him, since she didn't know much about him at all, but decided not to question it. Her dad was probably just being polite.

"Well, you two kids have fun watching your movie. I'm stepping out for a while to run some errands. Don't be a stranger, Viktor." He winked at Viktor, as if they shared some grand secret. As he passed by Alys and out the door, Viktor noticed that her gaze dropped to the floor.

Viktor said, "You okay?"

She nodded, lighting up once again after the door had closed.

Then Viktor said, "Your dad seems nice."

"Nice enough, I guess." She shrugged before tugging on

his sleeve, directing him down a short hallway. "Come on. The living room's this way."

Formal portrait paintings of what Viktor assumed to be family members hung on the walls. At the end of the hall to the left stood a large fern. To the right was a small table that served as home to a marble bust of a woman wearing a veil over her face. The living room was unlike any that Viktor had ever seen. The floor was sunken in the middle, and lining three-quarters of the circle was a sofa of sorts. In front of the couch sat a media console and television. On the oval coffee table sat two bottles of soda, a big bowl of popcorn, and a remote control. As they made their way down into the cozy television area, he cleared his throat and said, "So . . . that woman I saw leaving was your mom?"

Alys wrinkled up her nose. "Not even. She's sort of a protégé of my dad's. She spends quite a lot of time with us. But if you're wondering where my mom is . . . she died a long time ago."

Just hearing it sent a wave of empathy over Viktor. He couldn't imagine what it must be like to grow up having had a parent ripped from your life forever. He didn't want to imagine it. "I'm so sorry. That must be hard."

Alys plopped down on the couch and Viktor took a seat next to her. "It's not so bad. She died when I was little. I don't even remember her. Not really. I mean . . . there is this one memory I have of her. She was sitting on the porch of our house at the time, knitting a scarf. Funny the stuff you remember."

"It is." He squirmed a little, not knowing how to steer away from the subject or if he even should. "Are you close to your dad?"

Anything resembling a smile faded from her face. She was quiet for a long time, which struck him as odd. Was that something you needed to think about? Had he brought up something that had hurt or bothered her? His stomach felt like someone had just dropped a hot rock into it.

Alys flicked her gaze around the room, as if she didn't know where to look. At last, she met Viktor's eyes. "Can I tell you something? Just between us?"

He nodded. "You can tell me anything and I won't tell a soul. Promise."

All of a sudden, the house sounded dead silent—more so than it had just a moment before.

"Sometimes I feel more like his employee than his daughter, and it's a job that I can never quit. What's worse, if I don't do the job the way he wants me to, it's like he loves me less." Her words grew quieter as she spoke, as if this were the first time she had given voice to them and hearing them spoken frightened her. Shaking her head, she said, "It's stupid, right?"

"Not stupid at all. It sounds lonely." It had to be hard to be so alone, to feel like you had to earn your parent's affection and approval. Viktor didn't know what that must feel like. His parents had loved and supported him his entire life. At least . . . until recently. "Can I tell you something? Same rules?"

"Of course." She shrugged, drying tears that had not yet surfaced, as if she knew she was going to cry and felt the need to brush them away even though they didn't exist.

Viktor cleared his throat. When he spoke, his words were also hushed. It was only then that he realized that Alys's hand was on top of his own. "On the outside, it seems like my parents are awesome. Annoying, like parents usually are, but overall great. But . . ."

"But . . . ?"

"It's just that some things have happened lately that make me wonder if I even know them at all. Especially my dad. It's like I woke up one day and I live with people I don't even know. Maybe I never had. I'm not sure." His throat felt dry and the stone that had been in his stomach had found its way upward to his heart. He felt heavy.

They looked each other in the eyes then and held that gaze for a long time. "That sounds lonely too."

It *was* lonely. Viktor hadn't realized how lonely he'd been feeling until that moment. Yes, he could talk to Damon about it. But that didn't seem to ease the loneliness. "The truth is . . . I'm . . . kinda scared."

What was he scared of? Losing his family as he knew it. Losing his life. But most of all, losing his grip on what he'd known had been a core part of him—trust. He'd trusted his parents. What was he supposed to do now? How was he supposed to feel? And who on earth could he trust now?

"Me too." As Alys gave his hand a light squeeze, she said,

"But at least we're scared together."

Alys, he thought. He could trust Alys.

Clearing his throat, he said, "Can I tell you something else? Something I never tell anyone?"

"Of course." She scooched closer. "You can tell me anything."

"I don't have any friends. I mean . . . besides Damon." His voice caught in his throat for a moment.

"Well . . . you have one more now." She smiled into his eyes. "I'll be your friend, Viktor. For sure."

Some feeling flooded through him then, but he couldn't quite identify it. Joy, sadness, reassurance, relief? It was one of those. Maybe it was all of those. All Viktor knew was that tonight, he was a little less alone in the world.

Because Alys was there by his side.

His friend.

For sure.

CHAPTER SIXTEEN
Porch Ghosts and Vampire Stars

Viktor had hoped that his walk home that night would be full of grins and daydreaming about having kissed Alys, but that never happened. Instead, they'd watched the movie, laughed about the ridiculousness of the plot, and Alys walked him to the door. Still . . . he'd had a great time. He was thankful he'd met her, that they'd shared such personal feelings, that he had a new friend. It made him wonder if she'd shared stuff like that with other boys, or anyone for that matter, but he didn't really care if she had. The point was, she'd shared them with Viktor. And that was awesome.

As he reached his front porch, he was hit with the strangest, most unsettling feeling that he was being followed. Pausing, he turned around, scanning the yard, the street, as far as he could see, but there was nothing. Maybe his nerves were just on edge after the conversation he'd overheard his dad having with that Ruthven guy. In fact, he knew they were. How could they not be?

From the darkness came a whisper. "Viktor . . ."

Viktor's eyes went wide, but he didn't open the door and run inside. He couldn't. His feet were frozen to the porch in fear. He looked around, knowing the speaker was nearby. He didn't want to acknowledge the voice, but what else was he going to do while his sneakers were glued to the spot because he was terrified of a whisper? "Wh . . . who . . . who's there?"

"Viktor . . ." The whisper was louder this time, and Viktor began to wonder if maybe his porch was haunted by a ghost with laryngitis. "I'm coming, Viktor. I'm coming for you."

Viktor's heart pumped so fast that the sound of it pounded in his ears. Behind him the front door opened and a voice that he knew very well said, "Oh, honestly, Laura. You're going to give the boy a heart attack. Get in here."

Viktor turned around and in confusion said, "Aunt Carmilla?"

From the shadows beside the large hydrangea bush beside the porch came his aunt Laura, who was wearing an enormous grin. "Got ya!"

"Hello, Viktor. Where's my hug?" Aunt Carmilla hugged him then and he relaxed some, relieved that it hadn't been a porch ghost after all. As she released him, she placed a hand on his left cheek and smiled. "My goodness, you're growing so fast. I wish I could just freeze you in place."

"Ugh. He'd be stuck at twelve forever then, and what fun would that be?" Laura rolled her eyes, then she gave Viktor a playful slug in the shoulder. "Did I scare you?"

"I thought you were a ghost."

She tilted her head for a brief moment before saying, "A porch ghost?"

Viktor's eyes went wide. "How did you—"

Laura shook her head, dismissing her words almost the exact moment they'd left her lips. "It's not important. Come inside! Your mom's making lasagna."

"But she hates lasagna. She's allergic to garlic."

Aunt Carmilla said, "She's making it with shallots instead. Come. You must be hungry. It's getting late."

"Or early, depending on if you're a night person or not." For some reason, before heading back inside the house, Carmilla shot Laura a look that Damon would have referred to as a 'shut-up look'—something Damon's mom gave him on the regular. As if it just occurred to her that Viktor hadn't been home this entire time, Aunt Laura said, "Wait a second. Where were you before? With a girl maybe?"

Viktor shrugged. He liked sharing details of his life with his aunt Laura, but tonight had been special to him—something he wanted to keep for himself for a while, to wrap himself up in like a blanket when he needed a happy memory. "Just watching a movie with a friend."

"A *girl* friend? Or a girlfriend?" Laura winked at him,

but when met with Viktor's silence, she groaned and said, "Okay, okay, forget I asked."

They turned to go inside, but before they reached the door, Laura stopped in her tracks. She looked left and snapped, "What are you lookin' at, creeper?"

Viktor turned to see Celeste sitting on her front porch, watching the exchange between him and his aunt. When Laura spoke to her, Celeste shrank down in her seat. It was funny how his aunt had said the same thing to Celeste as she'd said to him a while ago. And awesome.

If Viktor didn't know any better, he might have thought his aunt was psychic. But psychics weren't real.

Were they?

Carmilla was just stepping into the kitchen by the time Viktor and Laura made their way inside. From the sound of it, his entire family was in there. With a deep breath, Viktor put on his best smile and went to join them. He had to fake it, after all. How was he supposed to sit there and manage an authentic smile when he was looking at his dad?

Mom was standing at the counter, cutting up various vegetables for a salad. Hannah was sitting at the table, playing with a tablet that must have been a gift from their aunts. Carmilla moved to sit beside her, and there, across from them, sat Viktor's father.

Dad smiled at Viktor, and when he did, his eyes sparkled. He didn't at all look like a man who was plotting to kill his own son. Maybe he wasn't one, Viktor thought. Maybe the entire thing was just a bad dream.

Dad said, "How was the movie?"

"It was all right. A little too mushy for my tastes. Not enough monsters or gore." Viktor shrugged. If he didn't know better, it would seem like his life was still the same as it always had been. "But then, I'm pretty certain that every movie can be improved with a little bloodshed."

His dad's smile broadened. "On that we agree."

Hannah was showing Aunt Laura something on her new tablet and Aunt Laura was giving her full attention, like she always did.

"Oh! I'd almost forgotten," Aunt Carmilla said. "Liz, I brought you some of that special bath oil that you love."

Mom looked over her shoulder at Carmilla with a grateful smile. "I didn't know you were in Romania."

Carmilla said, "Well, Romania adjacent, but still. I knew you'd appreciate it."

Dad chuckled. "Liz, darling, you know they have bath oil here, right?"

A giggle escaped her, and they shared a look that reminded Viktor how deeply his parents were in love. Maybe all the bad things he'd seen and heard really had been just a nightmare after all. Mom said, "Yes, but you can't even compare the two, my sweet."

"That reminds me." The smirk on his dad's face said everything as he turned to face his son. "Knock knock, Viktor."

Viktor paused, wishing more than anything he could sink into the floor. But then he'd be a floor ghost, he supposed. And everyone who's anyone knew porch ghosts were all the rage right now. He and Aunt Laura did, anyway. "Who's there?"

"Dwayne." His dad had sat forward some, as if he were about to share the best punch line ever.

Viktor groaned. "Dwayne who?"

"Dwayne the bathtub, I'm dwowning!"

Viktor rolled his eyes as Hannah burst out laughing—one of those laughs that bubbled up from deep within. "Good one, Dad."

His dad may or may not be a surreptitious, formerly-thought-to-be-a-monster, would-be mobster who put a hit out on his son, but he was still a dad, and the bad jokes were still flowing. Viktor couldn't figure out how his mom talking about bath oils had anything at all to do with a pathetic joke about drowning, but he'd accepted a long time ago that he'd never understand his parents. Adults were weird.

Mom withdrew two big wooden spoons from a drawer and began tossing the salad with some light dressing. "Hannah, help your brother set the table, would you?"

Viktor gathered the plates and glasses while Hannah laid out the silverware and napkins. As they worked, Hannah kept nudging her brother playfully and sticking out her tongue at him. Under his breath, Viktor said, "Ya butt," which made Hannah giggle, causing a natural smile to settle on Viktor's lips.

"How's school, Viktor?" Aunt Carmilla took a seat at the table and held up her glass for Dad to fill with wine for their meal. "Hannah caught me up on her experience earlier, but I'm curious about yours. Do you find the seventh grade challenging?"

Viktor nodded. "It's okay so far. I mean, Mom has me volunteering at the library, but that's okay too, I guess."

"Just okay?" Aunt Laura's brow furrowed in concern as she took a seat next to her wife.

Viktor wasn't sure what she was hoping for. It was middle school. Nothing about it was all that great. He shrugged. "Yeah, but it could be worse."

As Mom pulled the lasagna pan out of the oven, she said, "It's good to hear that attitude change."

He was careful to face away from his mom before rolling his eyes. He didn't have an attitude. He'd just been sentenced to the seventh grade and made his peace with it.

Aunt Laura had to cover her mouth to hide her grin.

"Oh, and I have a cool substitute teacher for English. We're reading *Dracula*."

Aunt Carmilla smiled. "Interesting choice. What do you think so far?"

He couldn't explain it, but suddenly it felt like all eyes were on him. All but Hannah's. "It's pretty cool, I guess. But the paper we're writing for English is supposed to describe what it would be like for a vampire to live in the modern age, and I'm having a hard time picturing it."

Aunt Laura cleared her throat. "Well, have you tried imagining yourself as a vampire? Like, maybe walk a mile in somebody else's coffin?"

"Laura . . ."

His dad sat forward. "Now hold on, Carmilla. I think your wife has a point. Ask yourself this, Viktor: if you were a creature who'd existed for centuries, how would you adapt to the present day?"

"I guess . . ." Viktor chose his words carefully, but it took a moment for him to speak them aloud. "I guess I'd lie a lot."

Dad glanced at Mom before nodding. "A fair answer, son. You might have no choice. Lying might just be the key to survival for such a being."

The rest of dinner, filled with conversation and laughter, passed by in a blink. Aunt Carmilla and Aunt Laura shared stories of their most recent travels. Hannah made up a silly story on the spot that even Viktor found funny. And Viktor regaled them with tales from his volunteer hours at the library. It was about as normal an evening as it could be.

But the words his dad had spoken about the need for a vampire to lie continued to echo in the back of his mind.

Later that night, after the house was dark and quiet, Viktor was lying on his bed, thumbing through his copy of *Dracula*. He heard a soft knock at his door and responded with, "Yeah?"

The door swung open, revealing his aunt Laura, who was holding a set of car keys in her left hand. "Well?"

Viktor blinked at her in confusion. "Well . . . what?"

"Are you comin' or not?"

Viktor dropped the book he was holding and sat up, grinning. "Where are we going?"

The corners of Aunt Laura's mouth turned up in a smile. "Trust me, Viktor. We have an important appointment to get to."

Minutes later, they were carefully buckled into Aunt Laura's car and speeding down the road at a rate that Viktor was quite certain his mother would not appreciate. Aunt Laura cranked up the volume on the radio, blasting "You're So Vein" by the Screaming Meemies. They sang along while Aunt Laura wound the rented red convertible through the streets of Nowhere, and soon Viktor realized that they were leaving Nowhere altogether.

The sign on the edge of town read "You are now leaving Nowhere. Come back soon!" As they passed it, Viktor watched a car drive past them, heading back into town as they were leaving it. The car's headlights were so bright that when the light struck his eyes, it almost hurt. Squinting, he said, "What are we doing?"

"I told you. We have an appointment."

"But . . . it's a school night," Viktor muttered, only slightly worried he sounded like his mom.

"Yes. And we have an appointment. . . ." Aunt Laura's

smile spread into a full-blown grin. She held up two concert tickets for him to see. "With the Screaming Meemies."

"You're kidding me!" Viktor snatched the tickets and read the printed text on them again and again. They were real, authentic tickets to a concert featuring his and Aunt Laura's favorite band.

"Viktor," she gasped in mock offense. "I don't kid about something as crucial as having parent-free fun. You know that."

Viktor grasped the tickets tight in his hands. There was no way he was going to risk losing them. Not when seeing the Screaming Meemies live was just a car drive away.

Not a chance.

An hour later they began passing large buildings as they made their way into the heart of the city—buildings Viktor didn't recognize, as he'd spent almost no time there at all. Mom and Dad preferred small-town life, which meant that he and Hannah were stuck "enjoying" small-town life. As Laura pulled into a parking lot, a prickly feeling crawled up the back of Viktor's neck. He'd never been to a nightclub before, and he was sure that if his parents found out, he'd be sentenced to mowing the neighbors' lawns for free for the rest of the summer. Being volun-told was bad enough. But forced labor, outside, under the heat of the summer sun? Viktor shivered at the thought.

On the far end of the lot stood a large warehouse. It was

old and looked like it had seen better days. The doors were covered in rust. Some panels of the arched windows had darkened with age, and several parts of the brick walls had been covered with graffiti. It was like any other old warehouse, and Viktor might not have noticed the building at all if his aunt Laura wasn't leading him toward it.

Viktor furrowed his brow in confusion as they reached the door. "I thought we were going to a nightclub. I may not be a party animal, but this looks like some old warehouse to me."

Laura grinned and pulled the door open. Music pumping with a heavy bass line poured out from inside. "It *is* some old warehouse. It's also a nightclub. You ready for this?"

Viktor nodded, but he wasn't sure he meant it.

The outside of the building may have looked like any old, worn-down warehouse, but inside was very different. Elements of the aged warehouse were everywhere, but the entire thing had been transformed into a club with a large stage at one end and a long bar lit up by neon lights on the other end. On the wall behind the stage were large marquee letters bearing what Viktor could only assume was the name of the club: The Vault. As Viktor took in the scenery, a thought occurred to him. "Can I even be in here? I mean . . . it's a bar, right? Don't I have to be older? Like . . . much older?"

"Relax, Viktor. It's an all-ages club." Aunt Laura chuckled, gesturing to the bar. "You thirsty? We still have a few minutes before the band takes the stage."

Viktor nodded, and once they had their drinks in hand, they made their way through a sea of people to a spot that Aunt Laura deemed acceptable. Viktor's heart was in his throat the whole time. Just as he was about to ask when the band would be taking the stage, the lights of both the room and the stage went off, painting every inch of the place in thick, black pitch.

Without warning, light poured from the spotlight above onto the lead singer of the Screaming Meemies, pooling him in a cool glow that intensified the paleness of his skin. His legs were clad in purple plaid skinny jeans that featured zippers on the thighs and a chain that hung on one hip. His boots were well-worn and military style. He wore a black T-shirt that read "I'm so goth I pee darkness." Two silver hoops pierced his bottom lip on one side—something Viktor had once heard referred to as a spider-bite piercing. The singer's eyes were lined with thick, black, messy eyeliner, and his nails were painted to match. His hair was pitch-black and fashioned in an emo style, his bangs hanging in his face some.

The singer stood there as the crowd howled and applauded, silent and waiting for something—what, Viktor had no idea. His hands were gripping the microphone stand, and when the crowd's noise quieted, he leaned into the mic and, with a calm, hushed voice that Viktor had memorized, said the catchphrase that was rumored to be the thing the band started every performance with. "You make me wanna scream."

The crowd erupted as the band went into one of their best-known tunes, "Bite Me, Baby." It took Viktor until the beginning of the second song before he realized that his cheeks were already hurting from grinning so much.

Viktor and Laura danced and sang along to every tune, and by the time the music stopped and the spotlight turned on again, once more illuminating the lead singer, Viktor's ears were ringing.

"Thank you!" the lead singer screamed. "I'm Sprat, and we are the Screaming Meemies. Good night!"

The stage went dark again, and the crowd went wild. Viktor's heart was pounding as he and Laura made their way to the bar. "That was amazing!"

Aunt Laura was beaming. "You think that was good? Just wait!"

"What do you mean?" He had no idea what his aunt was talking about—nothing could ever top that moment, he was certain—but he didn't have much time to think about it at all.

Aunt Laura smiled. "You'll see."

Then, from behind Viktor came a voice that said, "Hey, man. You're Viktor, right?"

Laura's grin stretched wide. She gestured behind Viktor with an encouraging nod.

Viktor turned and almost died from happiness on the spot. Sprat, the lead singer of the Screaming Meemies, the musician-slash-god who wrote the soundtrack to Viktor's emotional state on any given day, was standing right in front of him, and talking to him. On purpose. His throat didn't just feel raw from singing and shouting. It also felt dry from nervousness. So dry he could almost picture the skin cracking like sand. "Hey . . . yeah . . ."

With a brief glance at Laura, Sprat chuckled before turning his attention back to Viktor. "I just wanted to introduce myself. I'm—"

"Sprat." Viktor's adrenaline was still pumping from the concert, but his heart managed to beat just a little faster. "It is an honor to meet you. 'Shattered Pieces of My Soul,' 'Trash Can Panda Bear,' 'Safety Pin Surgery?' Some of my fave songs. You're a genius!"

Sprat smiled, his cheeks blushing. "Thanks. I just write and sing them, though. The guys do all the playing. That's the hard part."

Viktor shook his head. He couldn't even imagine himself standing onstage, belting out tunes that he'd written to hundreds of strangers. "I could never do what you do."

Shrugging, Sprat said, "Sure you could. If I can do it, pretty much anyone can."

"Not like you, though. Nobody can do it like you." He was fanboying and he knew it but didn't care.

"That's the thing, though, isn't it? Nobody can do anything like I can. Or like you can."

Laura was beaming with joy. "Thanks for taking a sec to say hi."

The smile on Sprat's face was endearing. Viktor was willing to bet that despite Sprat's onstage personality, despite some of the gloomiest, most heart-wrenching lyrics he wrote, Sprat smiled often offstage. "No prob. Happy to."

Viktor flicked his eyes back and forth between his hero and his aunt. "How do you two know each other?"

Laura said, "Oh, Sprat and I go way back. All the way back to when I used to babysit him."

Sprat chuckled. "Yeah, it's been a minute. But I've gotta tell you, the town of Bathory hasn't changed much since those days."

"That's a shame to hear. It could use some change."

"Bathory?" Viktor blinked. It sounded familiar, but he couldn't recall where he'd heard of it before.

Laura nodded. "Where we grew up. It's not far from Stokerton."

"So, my aunt Laura used to be your babysitter? That's just wild."

"You think that's wild? Someday I'll tell you about the night we used hair spray to make blowtorches." The smirk on Sprat's lips said it was very much a story that Viktor wanted to hear.

Laura's eyes went wide. "It's a long story, and not one I need my nephew repeating to his parents, thank you very much."

"Too long a story for tonight, but maybe next time we can hang out for a while and I'll tell you all the juicy details."

The look in Sprat's eyes said that he meant what he said. He'd hang out with Viktor in the future. Even though he was a god and Viktor was just some boring twelve-year-old.

Viktor was pretty sure he was dying from excitement. He made a mental note to check his pulse once their conversation was over. "That'd be amazing."

"I just wanted to say hi before the guys and I get our gear together. We've got a gig two states over tomorrow night, so I can't stay." Sprat gestured to the bartender, who handed him a small glass of blue liquid. A light-up cube was inside, giving it a cool glow. The rim of the glass was covered in something that looked like blue sugar.

Viktor said, "What's that?"

"It's a Pixie Stick. Nonalcoholic, of course. It's sweet, enough sugar in it to choke Willy Wonka, but *so* good. You want one?"

"Yeah!"

Sprat gestured to the bartender again and when the bartender slid a second glass across the bar, Sprat lifted his glass in a toast. "Here's to being yourself, no matter what." And they clinked glasses.

After they said their goodbyes, Viktor watched Sprat cross the crowded room to what looked to be the door to backstage, where a small group of people were waiting. After signing some autographs, Sprat opened the backstage door and when Viktor glimpsed who was inside, he gasped. She may have been dressed in a Screaming Meemies T-shirt and wearing lots more jewelry and makeup than he'd ever seen her wearing before, but he would have recognized his English teacher anywhere. He only glimpsed her for a moment, but October was talking to some of the guys from the band, looking like they were old friends. Holding her hand was a tall, broad-shouldered blond guy that he assumed to be her husband.

Viktor tore his gaze from the backstage door as it swung closed. Apparently, his teacher was even cooler than he'd realized. It was one thing to be a fan, but to hang out with the band . . .

Just like Viktor had tonight. All thanks to his aunt.

Aunt Laura's eyes lit up. "Wait here, Viktor. I have to go say hello to somebody."

Still floating after his conversation with Sprat, he nodded and watched as his aunt crossed the room and opened the door to backstage. He wasn't all that surprised to see Aunt Laura chatting with October before the door swung closed, but it shocked him to see the two women hugging when the drummer of the band opened the door again. After several minutes, Aunt Laura opened the door again to exit. When she did, Viktor's stomach flipped over several times in fear. Standing there behind his aunt, Viktor saw something on October that he'd never noticed before.

October had fangs.

Fangs. Like a vampire. Could that be real? Maybe it was just the lighting?

A minute later, his aunt appeared once again and walked back over to him wearing a smile. "You ready?"

He swallowed the growing lump in his throat and tore his gaze away from the backstage door. "Umm. Yeah. I guess I'm ready. For almost anything."

An hour later, just after two in the morning, they were passing the sign just outside of the town's boundaries that read "Welcome to Nowhere—somewhere to be." But before they reached the streets of Nowhere, Aunt Laura turned left and drove up a series of winding dirt roads until they came to a stop on top of the large hill that overlooked the town of Nowhere. They'd been here several times before and had the most amazing conversations. Aunt Laura wasn't just his aunt. She was his friend.

As they exited the car and climbed onto the hood once again, Viktor said, "I can't believe you know Sprat."

Aunt Laura's smile was big, but nowhere near as big as his. "Are your ears still ringing?"

Viktor still felt like he was floating from the high of the concert. He didn't ever want to come back down from the feeling. "A little. Worth it though."

Laura chuckled. "Sprat's nice, huh?"

"He was so cool. This is just the coolest night ever."

Aunt Laura was beaming. "I'm glad you had a good time."

"The best time." His thoughts drifted to how tense he'd felt lately. School was hard. Friends were harder sometimes.

And girls . . . well . . . Viktor paused for a long time before he spoke again. "Hey, Aunt Laura? If . . . if the friend who's a girl I mentioned earlier was . . . well . . ."

Laura smiled. "If she was someone you wish were more than a friend?"

He felt a blush cover his cheeks and thanked the darkness for hiding it. "Well . . . yeah."

"Just be yourself, Viktor. If she's worth your time, she'll see that you're worth hers."

He wasn't convinced that she was right, but still Alys touched on the edges of his thoughts. Alys and the library. Alys and the Tasty Cow. Alys and the couch at her house. Viktor sighed, gazing up at the night sky. "Wow. There are so many stars out tonight."

"You see that red one?" Laura pointed up, directing Viktor's attention to a bright red dot in the sky.

"That's a star?"

"Yep. It's rare. Astronomers call it R Leporis. It's known as 'a vampire's star.'" She smiled and Viktor wondered if she were remembering some special moment that was attached to the sight of that star, but he didn't ask. If she wanted him to know, she'd tell him on her own. As she lay back on the car, she said, "It's my favorite star."

Viktor let out a soft groan as he joined her in lying on the hood, taking in the wonder of the night sky. "What is it with vampires lately? It seems like they're everywhere."

"You mean, like rising from their coffins and walking

around?" She didn't look at him, but Viktor was pretty sure if she had, her eyes would've revealed just how dumb she thought he sounded.

He chuckled. "Nothing like that. It's just been a topic that keeps coming up a lot."

Turning her head toward him, she asked, "What do you think about them?"

"Vampires?" He thought about it for a moment before responding. "I dunno. I mean, I like the stories about them, but I wouldn't want to be one."

"Why not? All that power, cool fangs, never age . . ."

Above them Viktor spotted the Big Dipper, which was pretty much the only constellation he knew. "It just seems like it'd be kinda lonely, y'know? I've felt lonely enough lately. Don't need to add a thirst for blood to the situation."

She glanced at him, her eyes full of concern that she didn't put voice to. "What would you be? If you could be anything?"

It didn't take him long to come up with his answer. "Psychic."

"Oh? Why?"

"Because if I was psychic, I wouldn't have to wonder about anything. I would just know. I'd like that. Not being left in the dark so often about so much stuff."

She let out a wistful sigh, her eyes gazing up at the night sky. "I'd be that star."

They lay there, watching the sky in silence and wonder

for several minutes before Viktor spoke again. "Hey, Aunt Laura?"

"Yeah?"

Wetting his lips, he thought about his dad and said, "Can a person ever truly know another person?"

"Only if they're brave enough to let you." She released a sigh that was tinged with a sadness that Viktor wagered he couldn't understand. "And in my experience, people are rarely that brave."

As Viktor stared up at the vampire star, he wondered if his dad was brave enough to answer the questions that were burning within Viktor's mind. Questions that Viktor knew he had no choice but to ask him.

CHAPTER SEVENTEEN
Planet Viktor—Population: One

Viktor couldn't help but drum his fingers on his desk as he waited for October to return to room 31. For one, there was that whole my-teacher-may-actually-be-a-vampire thing he had to deal with. For two, he wanted to rehash how cool the Screaming Meemies concert had been with someone who'd understand. And for three, he'd finally managed in the wee hours of the morning to finish writing his paper on *Dracula*, which was due today. He wasn't thrilled with the way his essay had turned out, but it was done, so that was something. Teachers were always saying to turn something in—even if it wasn't his best work—so that was precisely what October was getting. Viktor's Okayest Work.

"Sorry I'm late!" Alys burst through the door with a frantic look on her face, but it fell to confusion when she found the teacher's desk empty. She blinked and looked around at the rest of the class. But when her eyes finally fell on Viktor, she visibly relaxed. Taking a seat beside him, she said, "They just transferred me to first period English from third period. Guess we're classmates now, huh?"

Viktor beamed.

A moment later, October slipped into the room with apologies. "Sorry I'm late, everyone. You can feel free to pass your essays to the front. I can't wait to see what you all came up with."

Without a word, Alys raised her eyebrows at Viktor, as if to say how relieved she was that she hadn't been caught coming in late. She moved down the aisle and took her seat, books clutched to her chest, content not to be noticed.

Viktor retrieved his essay from his messenger bag and saw that every other student had papers that looked to be two pages or more long. Viktor looked down at his almost-two-page essay and frowned. What could they say about Dracula living in the modern age that he hadn't said? That he'd be stuck in his old ways and resistant, but forced to change his diet?

Without warning, the image of his dad's favorite mug flitted through his mind—the one with a picture of a mosquito and the words "Careful! I bite." Shadowing that image was one of his dad reading from a paper newspaper and another of his dad wearing those hideous calf-length socks with his shorts from the eighties. Like Dracula, his dad was resistant to change, that was for sure.

But he wasn't a vampire. Viktor had already put that wild notion behind him. Hadn't he?

"All right, class. For the rest of the hour, we're heading down to the gym, where we'll all be educated and/or tortured by the likes of our guest, Sonnet Steve. Sonnet Steve is going to teach us all about Shakespeare . . . but with juggling." October didn't even try to fake excitement at the assembly news. She just sighed and said, "Sorry, guys. But hey, at least that means no homework, right? You can all head to the gym now. If you haven't passed your paper forward yet please drop it on my desk before you leave."

As the rest of the class shuffled out the door, Viktor approached October's desk with an eyebrow raised. "Sonnet Steve?"

"I know, right? You'd think the guy would have been more creative and gone with Bill Thy the Sonnet Guy or something. But . . . I'm sure it'll be fu—" She stopped herself before continuing in search of the right word to describe the assembly. Because by the look on her face, *fun* was not at all the word she'd been looking for. "Fine. It'll be . . . just . . . fine. I'm sure."

"Fine, maybe. But not fun. Not 'the Screaming Meemies concert in a cool warehouse nightclub' fun."

October's eyes went wide. "No way, you were there too?"

"My aunt surprised me with tickets. How'd you get backstage?"

"Suffice it to say, I've been besties with the lead singer since elementary school."

He leaned closer, keeping his voice hushed. "I saw you, with the . . ."

She raised an eyebrow at him. "With what?"

"I saw your . . . fangs." His stomach hurt, but he had no choice but to bring it up. Besides, October seemed so nice. What if she was the kind of vampire to not chomp on her friends and drink their blood? The least he could do is be supportive.

"Viktor! It was a Screaming Meemies concert. Didn't you look around? Ninety percent of the audience was wearing fangs!" With bemused laughter, October opened one of the drawers of her desk and pulled out a plastic box shaped like a coffin. Through the clear lid, Viktor could see a set of very realistic-looking fangs.

He felt like an idiot.

Alys set her essay on the teacher's desk. She was looking prettier than ever, with her hair drawn up in a ponytail tied with a black velvet ribbon. To his great delight, she was wearing a Screaming Meemies T-shirt. "Who got backstage where?"

Viktor said, "October got backstage with the Screaming Meemies."

"And I would love to regale you both with the tale, but you've got an assembly to get to." October pointed to the door.

Viktor and Alys exchanged looks before Viktor said, "If we promise to wash the whiteboards, can we stay and hear more?"

October laughed. "Nice try, guys. Sonnet Steve is waiting."

Later that day, Viktor wasn't even sure anymore if the books he was returning to the library shelves were in the right section, because he'd been lost in thought over Alys and whether Aunt Laura was right about Alys seeing that he was worth her time. He couldn't imagine any girl thinking of him that way, but then, he'd always kinda thought that no girl would ever like him the way that he liked them. Not that he'd liked many girls, of course. He could count all of the girls he'd liked in his twelve years on planet Earth on one hand. If he were talking to Damon about it, it'd be on three fingers. But if he were honest . . . there was just Alys. The first, one, and only girl who'd ever made his heart blow up like a balloon.

He was terrified it might pop.

"Viktor . . ."

Of course, there was the terrifying possibility that Alys didn't think of him the same way he thought about her at all. What if he told her that he had a crush on her, just to hear her laugh at the very idea of being his girlfriend? But then, why did she hold his hand if she didn't like him the same way that he liked her? What did it mean?

"Oh, Viktor . . ."

He volunteered in a library. Weren't there any books in this place that could help him? Maybe something like *Dr. Bob's Guide to Preteen Girls*? Or *How I Got the Girl: One Tween Guy's Helpful Step-By-Step*?

Of course, it would probably help him more to ask a girl about how to interact with girls, but who would he even ask?

"Viktor, are you even listening to me?"

Blinking, Viktor turned his head to see Mrs. Conrad standing at the end of the row with one hand on her hip and a bemused smile on her face. "Off on Planet Viktor again, eh? Anything I can help with? Or are you just lost in thought over your reasons why you're putting horror books away in the nonfiction section? Some parents might take issue with that."

Planting his feet back on Earth, he started taking the books he'd placed there off the shelf and back onto the cart again. With a snort, he said, "Any parent who thinks kids can't handle horror has clearly never experienced middle school gym class, that's for sure."

Mrs. Conrad chuckled and shook her head. "You aren't wrong about that. Would you mind handling the desk for a while? You can put these away later."

She tilted her head, a look of concern on her face. "Is something bothering you, Viktor? Are you okay?"

"I'm fine, Mrs. Conrad. I'm just"—the bell on the front door jingled, and when Viktor looked to see who was coming inside, his heart shot into his throat—"distracted."

"By what, if I may ask?" Mrs. Conrad narrowed her eyes in confusion before looking behind her at the girl who'd just entered the library. With an understanding smile, she turned back to Viktor. "Oh, I see. Not a what. But a who."

"She's just—"

"Have fun, Romeo." After chuckling, she snapped her fingers and said, "Speaking of which, Taylor owes a fine on that big Shakespeare collection. Don't let him check anything else out until he returns it and pays up, okay?"

"No problem."

"And Viktor?"

"Yeah?"

"Wanna hear a secret?" She was whispering, but in that loud way people sometimes did when they were joking that they were trying to keep quiet without actually doing it. After he nodded, she said, "Talking to girls isn't as complicated as you might think. Just be nice, show her some respect, and let her get to know the real you."

He smiled. "Thanks, Mrs. Conrad." *But that*, Viktor thought, *would require me to have some kind of idea who the real me is.*

He made a mental note to figure it out at some point, but he was pretty sure he was going to ignore that note the same way he'd ignored his grade in English last year. That is, pretend it's nothing to worry about until things got dire and life as you knew it was on the line.

"Hey, Viktor. Can you check me out?"

Realizing what she'd said, he blushed. Of course, she'd meant that she wanted him to check some books out for her, but Viktor was checking her out in a whole other way.

"Oh, hey . . . Alys." He swallowed hard, trying to come off sounding cool and casual. As every second passed, it became quite clear that the dry lump in his throat caused by just the sight of her wasn't going anywhere anytime soon. "Cool shirt. Y'know, October wasn't the only person there. I just saw them in concert with my aunt."

Alys's eyes went wide with wonder. "You did? I'm so jealous! What was it like? I've heard that some bands aren't so great live."

"They were amazing. I met Sprat." Sure, he was bragging a little. But it couldn't hurt to share some impressive details with her, which might make her think that he was way cooler than he actually was.

"You're kidding! He's incredible! You have to tell me everything. I need to know every single detail."

Mrs. Conrad's advice about showing a girl who he really was floated through his mind, and he cleared his throat. "My aunt set it up. She surprised me. Sprat was cool, though. I saw October there—she apparently knows Sprat too. I think I mumbled and acted like an idiot the whole time I was talking to him."

"I bet you were awesome." The corners of her mouth lifted in a small smile—one that was beginning to make

Viktor feel dizzy in the best kind of way. "What's your favorite song of theirs?"

"There are too many to just choose one."

"I know what you mean. Last week I was obsessed with 'Break My Art, Break My Heart,' but this week I can't get enough of 'Clown Killer.'"

"Don't forget 'Spiderweb Skull.'"

"Oh, man, I forgot about that one." Their eyes locked in a gaze that Viktor never wanted to be released from. But after a moment, she said, "So . . . about checking me out . . . I have a book waiting for me at the front desk, I think."

"No prob." Walking her back to the front desk, he noticed the book she was talking about sitting right beside the computer monitor and began typing the book's information into the computer. "*Terrence Blomberg's Big Book of Whittling*, eh? What are you whittling?"

Shrugging, she said, "Nothing much. Just some wood stuff."

"I imagine that's a prerequisite to the craft."

Laughter bubbled up from inside of her. It sounded so natural. Viktor could have gone on listening to it forever—even if that meant never hearing a song by the Screaming Meemies ever again. When her laughter melted into a sparkle in her eye, she said, "I had a great time the other night, by the way."

"Me too." He tried to wet his lips, but it seemed all the moisture in his body had evaporated at the sight of her.

"Maybe . . . maybe we could . . ."

"You read my mind. I was just thinking that maybe we could do it again sometime." When his response was stunned silence, she picked up the book and headed for the door with a grin. "Thanks for the book."

"Anytime." Summoning up every ounce of bravery that he could, Viktor said, "And hey, if you ever wanna get together to listen to the Screaming Meemies . . ."

She opened the door, and just before she stepped outside, she offered him a wink and said, "I know just who to call."

A moment later, the door swung shut behind her, and Viktor melted into a puddle of goo on the library floor.

CHAPTER EIGHTEEN
A Disagreement of Sorts

Later that afternoon, once he was home again, Viktor steeled himself for a conversation that he didn't know how to start. He'd practiced a few possible opening words, but none of them felt quite right to him. As he made his way downstairs, he decided that the best way to begin was, as with most things, simply to begin.

Truth be told, he'd been feeling much more confident about having this conversation before he learned that he'd been completely wrong about October.

He spied his dad through the front bay window, a rake in his hand. His dad wasn't doing any yard work. Instead, he was staring across the street, his eyes locked on the woman who lived with Abraham and Alys. In return, the woman was staring back. Neither appeared very happy. In fact, if Viktor didn't know better, he would have thought that his dad was threatening her with just a look. Like two cats that had noticed one another and did not approve of the scenario one bit.

With a deep breath, Viktor stepped out the front door. "Dad? Can I talk to you? It's import—"

"Not now, Viktor."

"But Dad—"

"Not now!" Dad's words were biting. He tore his gaze from the woman for a moment and looked at Viktor, an apology lurking in his eyes. "Go back inside, son. Lock the doors."

Viktor's throat felt dry. It was clear that something was very, very wrong, but he couldn't discern what. "Why?"

"Just do it." On the surface, Dad's tone seemed calm, but something about his posture said that he was anything but.

Without another word, Viktor made his way to the front door, glancing back at his dad every couple of feet, wondering once more what was happening. It occurred to him that Aunt Laura had been right. You can't know a person unless they're brave enough to share with you who they are. And his dad hadn't been brave Viktor's entire life.

Viktor didn't know his dad. Not really. He'd heard stories from his parents about their lives before children, but it had always seemed like those stories were missing something. He just hadn't recognized what. But now he did.

Depth. The stories he'd been told had been missing depth.

Who was Drake Valentine?

As Viktor closed the front door behind him, his mom

called from the hallway, "Viktor, give me a hand, will you?"

She was standing on her tiptoes in front of the hall closet, trying to pull a plastic bin down from the top shelf. Viktor didn't think he'd be much help—she was taller than he was—but when Mom says to help her, you help her. Together they got the bin down and set it on the floor. It was heavier than he thought it would be, and he had a passing curiosity of what was in it.

"Mom, something's up with Dad. He told me to come inside and lock the doors."

"What?" Mom's eyes went wide as she met his gaze. "Where is he?"

A strange prickly feeling had crawled up the back of his neck. Something *was* wrong.

"Viktor, where is your father?" Her voice took on an urgent tone.

"In the front yard." As she moved to the front window and peered outside, Viktor said, "What is it?"

"He's not there anymore. Did he say anything?" She hurried to the front door and locked it. As she made her way to the back door in urgent steps, Viktor followed.

"He just told me to get inside and lock the doors. What's going on?"

She turned the dead bolt on the door, clicking the lock in place. "Nothing your father can't handle, I'm sure. Why don't you go to Hannah's room and keep her entertained for a little while?"

"Mom." He placed a hand on her shoulder to get her attention. When she looked at him, he kept his tone calm, even though he was feeling anything but. "Tell me what's happening."

She searched his eyes, as if debating how much to share with him. But just as she parted her lips to respond, the front door flew open despite the engaged lock and Dad hurried inside. Mom cried out, "Drake! Are you all right?"

The front of Dad's shirt was covered in blood, glistening crimson against pale blue cotton. The sight of it sent Viktor's heart in a terrifying rhythm. He could smell it even from a distance—there was that much of it. Rotten pennies, metallic and bitter.

Dad stumbled forward, and Mom rushed to him in a panic. "It's okay," he said between panted breaths. "It's not all mine."

Viktor watched as Mom looked over Dad's neck, chest, and stomach for injuries. Dad's chest was rising and falling in quick, urgent breaths. From where Viktor was standing, he couldn't see any cuts. But the sight of the blood made the room tilt. Viktor's stomach roiled. "Then whose is it?"

As if just then realizing that Viktor was in the room, Dad blinked and offered a dismissive sigh. "I was just joking, Viktor."

His dad was lying to him. First hiding things. Then meeting in secret with a strange man. Now lying. When would it end? When would Viktor learn the truth? "No. I know when you're joking and that wasn't it. Whose blood is on your shirt, Dad? What is going on?"

Mom spoke to Viktor in a matter-of-fact tone. "Go keep an eye your sister."

"Mom, I'm not—"

"Viktor!" The inflection of his dad's voice said that he'd had enough. Just hearing it shook Viktor to his core. His dad had never yelled at him prior to this day, and he'd done so twice in the past ten minutes. Without apology and without softening the sharp edges on his words, Dad said, "Listen to your mother. Go upstairs and keep Hannah in her room and calm until we call for you."

Viktor looked at each of them and then, shaking his head, he left the room. But he didn't go upstairs. Hannah was fine in her room, and his being there with her wouldn't make her any more okay than she already was. Instead, he stood around the corner, tucked away just inside the den, and listened to his parents' conversation.

His mom waited until she was relatively certain that Viktor was out of earshot before speaking—her voice quiet and subdued. "I thought you'd changed your mind about all of this. I thought you were going to leave it be."

With a hurried tone, he tried to reassure her. "I had. I was."

"Then what happened?"

"You know what happened. What always happens." Dad sounded defeated. Exhausted, even. What had transpired in the few minutes that he'd been outside and Viktor had been inside talking to his mother? Whatever it was, it was anything but good.

With a sigh, she said, "This has to end, Drake. You can't go on like this forever. *We* can't."

"I know." He took a breath and called out, "Viktor . . . it does no good for you to lurk. Come in here. It's time we had a talk."

Steeling himself, Viktor returned to the living room. He stood in front of his dad for a few breaths before gesturing to his dad's bloody shirt and saying, "Are you all right? Do you need to go to the emergency room?"

"I'm fine. Nothing your mother can't patch up with a simple stitch or two." He tried offering a comforting smile, even though the look in his eyes said that he knew that Viktor wouldn't accept the smile as real.

Mom was looking back and forth between the two of them with hesitation in her eyes. At last, she said, "I'll get the med kit. We need to clean that wound and treat it right away. Will you boys be okay without me for a minute?"

Dad caught her hand in his and placed a soft kiss on it, holding her gaze. "We'll be fine, darling."

Once his mom was out of the room, Viktor looked at his dad and said, "What happened to you?"

His dad wet his lips, choosing his words with great care. "A disagreement of sorts."

"Well, it looks like somebody disagreed with you on

whether your blood should be inside of your body or out."

His dad nodded. "Yes, well . . ."

Mom returned with the first aid kit and, after lifting Dad's shirt, began dabbing the edges of the wound with gauze. Dad winced at one point, but when he spoke, Viktor could detect no notes of pain in his voice. "Liz, as soon as Carmilla and Laura get back from the store, I want you to take Hannah and them and go somewhere far away from here."

As she reached for a bandage, her movements slowed. "Is this a conversation we should be having right now?"

Dad waited a beat and then replied, "Yes. I believe it is."

She looked at him, her eyes pleading. "But . . . what about Viktor?"

Viktor looked at his mom and asked, "What about me?"

Dad spoke as if Viktor weren't even in the room, but the look he gave his son as he spoke to his wife said he was trying hard to reassure them both. "He's old enough to know. He was old enough three years ago. It's time he learns about our situation. Ignorance can only harm him at this point."

"I agree," Viktor said, before taking a deep breath and continuing. "I'm right here, y'know. You guys can talk to me."

"Of course. We're sorry, dear. It's just that . . . we're in a delicate situation." Her tone changed then, making it clear that she wasn't happy with her husband at the moment. "And your father seems to think he can handle it all on his own."

Dad shook his head. "That's not true."

"The wound on your chest says otherwise." As if she'd forgotten about Viktor's presence, she continued. "Has it occurred to you that it's a good bet that many of us could face off with just some of them? It's possible that we could—"

"It has occurred to me, but . . ." Dad drew in a deep breath then, as if gathering the strength to continue his sentence. "Liz, I sent word to Lilith and requested her aide."

There was a beat of silence, but to Viktor, it felt like the moment dragged on for hours. His mother broke the silence at last. "You did what?!"

His dad's words were subdued with an apology it was clear he wasn't certain his wife would ever accept. "I had no choice. Can't you understand that? So yes, I made the decision on my own and summoned Ruthven. I gave him a letter for Lilith explaining everyth—"

"No, I can't understand it. How could you do something so *reckless* without even discussing it with me? We've always supported one another, listened to one another, made choices based on our collective wants and needs. This . . . this is an enormous betrayal, Drake. I can't even begin to find the words to describe how livid I am with you right now!"

Dad's voice cracked a little. "I'm sorry. I thought I was making the right decision. For me. For us. But I was wrong. I see that now. I just hope you can forgive me one day."

"If we survive this, you mean." Her words were almost a growl. Viktor couldn't recall a time when he'd ever seen his mom so mad. "How could you, Drake? How could you do that? Lilith, of all people. You know what she is. What she does. Summoning her here . . . you've endangered our family. Our children!"

"That's why I want you and the girls to leave. Please, Liz. Do this for me."

"How am I supposed to abandon you in a situation like this? To Lilith's will?" She sighed. "Even if I can manage to convince Laura to leave with Hannah and me, it'll be damn near impossible to convince Carmilla."

With urgency, Dad said, "Don't mention Lilith to them. If you do, Carmilla will insist on staying and . . . I just can't have that."

Mom's voice was shaking as she gestured to Viktor. "And our son?"

His dad was quiet. He met Viktor's eyes, as if to reassure Viktor that what he was about to say was true. "He'll be okay."

"I should be there, Drake. You can't do this alone." Mom's tone was warm once again. She was worried. Mad as hell, but worried and wanting to help however she could.

"No, darling. Please. Just go. Be safe for me. For our family."

"I swear, if Viktor gets hurt—"

Dad shook his head. "He won't. I'll protect him."

Pointing at Viktor with a commanding finger, she said in a no-nonsense Mom tone, "You listen to everything your father says. Do whatever he tells you to and don't argue. You hear me?"

Viktor's chest felt tight. "Yeah, Mom. I hear you. I don't understand, but—"

"Your father will explain everything." Fighting back tears, she added, "I need to help Hannah get her things together."

As Mom went upstairs, Viktor could swear he heard her crying. Dad took his time before speaking again. After a long pause, his dad said, "Viktor, there are things about me that I haven't shared with you. I was trying to protect you and your sister. But now I see I've done you a serious disservice by keeping certain things from you. I cannot tell you how sorry I am for that."

Viktor set his jaw, angry that Dad had made Mom cry. Angry that Dad had kept secrets from him . . . and that Mom had too. "You could start by explaining to me what you're talking about and holding your apology until the end."

"Dad, are you okay?" Hannah had appeared at the bottom of the stairs, her wide eyes, shimmering with the threat of tears, locked on their dad's bloodstained shirt, her bottom lip quivering. Seeing her so frightened made Viktor's blood boil with more anger. He'd always been protective of his sister, but knowing that it was their dad's fault that she was looking as scared as she ever had made him want to grab their dad and shout at him to fix this—whatever it was. No more secrets. No more lies.

Dad's smile came easy. "I'm fine. I just cut myself when I was fixing Mr. Thompson's lawn mower, that's all. But your mom stitched me up and I'll be all healed before you know it."

Hannah stepped forward with obvious hesitation but managed to make it all the way to where Dad was sitting. "That's a lot of blood."

"It looks like more than it is."

Hannah looked wary. Viktor wondered if Mom had any idea that Hannah was downstairs at all.

"Do you know where your suitcase is, sweetheart?" Dad's tone was dismissive, but in a way that told Viktor that Dad was trying to distract Hannah. By the look on Hannah's face, it wasn't working, but she played along.

"The pink one that Aunt Carmilla got me for my birthday?"

Dad nodded. "That's the one."

"It's under my bed." She flitted a glance at Viktor—one filled with countless questions. He wished he had answers to provide her.

"Can you go get it and help your mom pack?"

Hannah tilted her head as she asked, "Are we going somewhere?"

"Not all of us, but you, your mom, and your aunts are going to take a fun trip somewhere. A girls trip!" He turned some and winced at the pain that he was feeling from the wound they were all pretending he didn't have. "Just . . . go get your suitcase and start packing, okay? Don't forget your toothbrush."

Without another word, Hannah turned and moved up the stairs again, but not before shooting Viktor a look that said she wanted to know what was going on when he got a chance to tell her.

As soon as Hannah was out of sight, Viktor wasted no time. "Dad, are you in the mafia?"

Dad's eyes went wide for a moment. "What? No. No, nothing like that. Really, Viktor. Things like that belong in the movies."

Viktor felt his chest tighten with determination. "I saw you the other night, Dad. I heard you talking to that man in the red suit—Ruthven."

"Oh." A look of genuine surprise crossed over his dad's face. "Did you now?"

There was a distinct pause—one that hung heavy in the air between them.

"He's a very old friend from a very long time ago."

"Okay, but what about Lilith?"

The corner of his dad's mouth twitched, but Viktor couldn't be certain if it was because Viktor was pressing him with questions, or because the very mention of Lilith's name irritated him so.

"Lilith is . . . well . . ." Dad glanced down at his shirt, his eyes lingering there, his focus on the drying blood. "She's *not* a friend to me—or to anyone at all, really."

"Who wants you dead? Why? Whose blood is that on your clothes?" The questions were coming easier now. It was as if a dam had burst inside of him, and the questions were just pouring out.

His dad sighed. "Viktor, I know you have a million questions, and you will have answers, I assure you. But now is a time for planning."

"I want to know where Mom and Hannah are going."

Dad met his eyes. "We can't ask them that. We can't know where they're going. It's not safe for us to know. Now . . . go help your mom get their bags in the car, please."

"Dad, I'm not leaving this room until you tell me what's going on."

"Viktor!" He took a deep breath and blew it out again, centering himself, getting his temper under control. "I need you to keep calm. We'll get through this okay if we keep our heads. All right?"

Viktor nodded. "All right. But I will get answers. You owe me that much."

"And so much more, son." Darkness clouded his dad's eyes then. A sad storm. With hints of anger. "You have no idea how much more I owe you than that."

The shiver that crawled up Viktor's spine at that moment was almost painful.

CHAPTER NINETEEN
Infamous Last Words

Outside the sun was shining. The sky was robin's-egg blue. Birds were chirping in the trees and the soft hum of a lawn mower could be heard in the distance. It was, on the surface, a pristine day in the town of Nowhere, but underneath that, something darker lurked—something that had Viktor's stomach tied in knots as he helped load the suitcases into the trunk.

Aunt Carmilla's lips had been pressed in a thin, angry line ever since she returned to their house and Mom filled her in. She was upset with Dad, upset with the whole situation, and Viktor had a feeling that his aunts and parents were all privy to a huge chunk of information that they'd yet to share with him. Aunt Laura had been quiet, but when she spoke, it was in soft, pleasant tones to Hannah—perhaps to keep her calm.

"Drake, this whole so-called solution of yours is madness," Carmilla said, as Dad closed the trunk. "Together we may be able to fend off Lilith. To send us all away makes no sense whatsoever."

Viktor picked up Hannah's suitcase and placed it in the trunk, frowning.

"It makes perfect sense. Are you telling me you've forgotten what happened the last time we dealt with Lilith? It's a wonder Liz and Laura survived. I can't have that again, Carmilla. I won't. I need you to protect them. To protect Hannah as well. Please tell me you can do this for me. I'm begging you." Dad quieted his voice, as if that would keep Viktor from hearing him, even though Viktor was standing just three feet from them, playing luggage Tetris. "I can resist her so-called charms, but few can. Help me. Please."

Carmilla didn't bother to quiet her voice. "What about Viktor? Are you so certain he'll be able to resist?"

What about Viktor? seemed to be a theme for the day. Viktor rolled his eyes. It seemed like the only person who wasn't wondering about him was, well, him.

"He'll be fine." Dad glanced at Viktor, then spoke in a normal voice, giving up the hope of secrecy. "I need him to take care of the girl while I deal with our friend. Then, after our task is finished, we can get away before Lilith even shows up."

"This is perhaps the most stupid you've ever been, Drake." Aunt Carmilla shook her head. "I'll protect them. Just . . .

watch out for Viktor. He has no idea what he's about to walk into."

Understatement of the year, thought Viktor.

Dad said, "My hope is that he never will."

"If that's your hope, you're more reckless than I thought." Carmilla cast Viktor a look that said she was worried. More than that, that she was scared. "Tell him, Drake. Tell him everything."

"I will. Soon."

"We're all set here."

Viktor looked at the last suitcase and back at the trunk. He wasn't sure what Mom was talking about. They might be all set, but not so much the luggage.

To Viktor's relief, Dad shifted two of the suitcases in the trunk and slid the last one in without so much as a moment of hesitation, closing the trunk. When he turned back to Mom, he said, "Call me in the morning, all right?"

"I will." Mom's eyes shimmered. Behind her, Aunt Laura was helping Hannah buckle in while Aunt Carmilla slid into the front passenger seat. Mom's voice cracked when she said, "Please be careful, my love."

Dad placed a small, soft kiss on her forehead. Viktor couldn't be certain, but he thought he saw tears in his dad's eyes. "I love you, Countess."

"I love you too." She dried her eyes as she opened the back driver's side door and slid in next to Hannah. Viktor watched as Aunt Laura backed out of the driveway and drove down the street, not knowing where they were going or why, just that they were going, and that he and Dad had been left there to deal with . . . something.

It only took minutes to watch them leave and for Viktor and his father to cross the street, but it felt like hours. Dad hadn't even bothered to change into a clean shirt before guiding Viktor across the street. Nor had he bothered to explain whose blood it was. He moved with a purpose that Viktor didn't understand. When they came to a stop in front of Alys's house, Viktor was even more confused. "Dad, what are we doing here?"

His dad wasn't looking at him. In fact, he hadn't laid eyes on Viktor since the moment they'd left their house. Instead, he was looking up at the house as if this trip were long overdue. "We're here to visit a friend."

Viktor was overwhelmed with confusion. Did his dad even know Alys? "A friend? I didn't think you'd met the new neighbors yet."

"Oh, I've met them. Two of them, anyway."

Viktor raised an eyebrow. "You sure you wanna say hi with all that gore on your shirt?"

But his dad had fallen silent. He wondered if maybe Alys would believe it if he told her that they'd been making jam and a jar had exploded.

Ignoring Viktor's question, his dad stepped up onto the porch. Viktor looked at him, *really* looked. He tried hard to see the man he'd become convinced was dangerous, but it was difficult. All he could see was the man who'd taught him how to ride a bike; the man who'd helped him study for countless exams; the man who'd made him laugh more times than he could count and roll his eyes at his terrible jokes ten times more than that.

Dad raised his fist to the door and after a moment of hesitation, knocked loudly. They stood in silence as they waited for someone to answer—Viktor looking at his dad and Dad looking at the door. A horrifying thought occurred to Viktor, and his stomach twisted into knots. What if they were here to hurt Alys?

The door swung open, revealing Alys's father. He was dressed in the same style outfit he'd been wearing the night Viktor had met him, but now in a palette of grays. The expression on his face suggested he'd been waiting for them to show up—or rather, for Viktor's dad to show up.

"Good evening, Drake."

Dad offered a curt nod. "Abraham."

Viktor furrowed his brow in confusion. Not only had he had no idea that they knew each other, but he couldn't figure out why Abraham hadn't asked right away why the front of Dad's shirt was caked in blood. Not to mention the added weirdness that neither of them had so much as glanced in Viktor's direction.

Abraham looked down at Dad's shirt, as if it were a normal sight to see dried blood on Dad's clothing, and met his eyes again. In a tone that mirrored one that someone would use to tell someone else that their fly was down, Abraham said, "I see you're wearing what remains of my protégé. Nice of you to dress for the occasion."

Images of the woman Viktor had seen coming in and out of Alys's house filled Viktor's head. So that was who his dad had hurt. But was she just hurt? Was she dead? Abraham's chosen words suggested that she'd been killed and all that was left of her clung to the cotton on Dad's chest. So it was true. His dad *had* killed someone. And Abraham was oddly flippant about the entire situation.

Viktor's chest grew so tight it felt like his ribs were trying to crush his lungs into a pulp.

Abraham opened the door wide. "Come in."

Dad didn't hesitate, but it took Viktor a moment to choose between running away and stepping into the house. It felt strange, standing there in the foyer, not knowing why his and Alys's dad seemed to not care for each other a bit—especially having not known that they were acquainted. It was stranger still to know that they were here for a reason that, while unknown to Viktor, carried a weight of finality to it. Whatever it was, it had been a long time coming. And now Viktor was right in the middle of it—whatever it was.

In a similar tone as their host's, Viktor's dad responded with, "She attacked me. I had no choice."

The corner of Abraham's mouth twitched. "Oh, I think you did have a choice. But you have a history of choosing poorly."

Dad's jaw tightened. Whatever this was, it was the remnants of a long, ongoing argument between them.

Viktor glanced at the door, reconsidering his decision to enter the home. He could still run, just bolt out the door and sprint straight to Damon's house, call the police, and hope that his life wouldn't be as shattered after that as he imagined it would. But then, by the conversation Dad and Mom had been having earlier, it sure sounded like Mom was at least partially aware of what was going on. And if that were true, it meant that Dad would get arrested and so would Mom. What would happen to him then? To Hannah? As much as he hated the decision, he opted to stay and see this through. Sometimes there are just no good options to choose from.

Relaxing his jaw once more, Dad said, "Just because you disagree with a decision that I make doesn't make it the wrong choice."

Abraham clucked his tongue as he shut the door behind them, sealing them inside. The slight echo of Abraham's voice as he spoke reminded Viktor of a tomb. "There you go again—not understanding the difference between right and wrong. Despite what you may believe, Drake, life is made of clear choices, black and white, good and bad. It's your refusal of that that's brought you to this moment."

Despite the fact that his ribs were still squishing his lungs as hard as they could and fearing that his lungs may pop at any second, Viktor piped up, "What moment is that?"

"Viktor." Abraham looked at him with surprise, as if just then noticing they weren't alone. "It's good to see you again. Alys has stepped out for a bit, I'm afraid."

He sounded so casual, as if this were just one set of neighbors dropping by to borrow a cup of sugar from another neighbor, rather than a bloodstained archenemy and his tag-along son. Adults were weird.

"I—that's okay. I don't think we're here to see her anyway." He hoped not. The last thing Viktor needed was to add the girl he liked to the mix. It was bad enough that her dad was involved. That his dad was involved.

Viktor's stomach tightened in solidarity with his lungs.

"To be frank, it's for the best that she's not here." Dad locked eyes with Abraham. "I'd hate for her to get hurt."

Viktor looked from his dad to Abraham, a sick feeling spreading through his insides.

Bemused, Abraham shook his head, a small smile touching the corners of his mouth. "Oh, Drake. I have missed your sense of humor."

With a lack of sincerity, Dad said, "I wish I could say the same."

Ouch. Archenemy vibes or not, that had to hurt. At least on some level.

Abraham turned his attention back to Viktor and said, "So tell me, Viktor, to satisfy my undying curiosity—are you like your father? Taking over the family business, so to say?"

"Family business?" He furrowed his brow. "I'm not sure I

know what you're talking about. Do you mean coffin-building?"

Abraham raised an eyebrow and turned his attention back to Viktor's father. "Ohhh . . . does Daddy have a secret? Shame on you, Drake. Fathers should never lie to their children."

Viktor scowled. What was his dad lying about—apart from omitting details of how all that blood got on his shirt? And why did Abraham seem to know what it was?

"No. They shouldn't." Viktor's dad looked at Abraham and a long silence passed before he spoke again. "I wonder how much you've shared with your daughter. Ironic, isn't it, that she and my son managed to cultivate a friendship, considering our shared history?"

Abraham smiled, a hint of sinister pride. "You thought that was a coincidence?"

Growing tired of being made to feel no more relevant than the plant in the corner, Viktor cleared his throat and said, "Dad, what is this? Why are we here?"

A heavy silence grew between them—one that Viktor was not at all surprised by. It was clear this conversation had been brewing for a long time between his dad and Abraham. What was not clear was his dad's need for Viktor's presence.

Abraham snapped at Dad then—a strange, angry shadow passing over him. Something in the air had shifted, and the time for pleasantries was gone. "Old friend, if you don't tell him your dirty little secret, I will."

"*Old friend.*" Dad shook his head. He looked both taken

aback and insulted. "How dare you come here to do as we both know you plan to and refer to me as *old friend.*"

"Tell him the truth, Drake. Now."

Dad dropped his gaze to the floor in defeat, the heaviness of his secret weighing him down.

Viktor's heart ached at the sight of his dad so upset. He glanced at the drying stain on his dad's shirt and wondered what could be so much worse that his dad would hesitate to share it with him. "What is it, Dad? I want to know the truth. Whatever it is."

"Viktor, I want to tell you everything. I just . . . don't know how to tell you." His dad's tone shifted from a voice of strength to one of contrition. His words faded into near whispers. "But it's long overdue."

Abraham's words were sharp, slicing through the air without apology. "Be grateful I'm letting you share word of your affliction, Drake. Think of this confession as your famous last words."

Viktor flicked his eyes between his father and Abraham. Did that guy seriously just threaten his dad's life? *No,* Viktor thought. *The look on his face says that it wasn't a threat. It was a promise.*

"It's not an affliction, Abraham. How many times must I explain to you that I'm not ill?" Dad held Abraham's gaze for a moment, letting his words soak in, but Abraham seemed less than convinced.

"How can you not comprehend that it's a virus, old

friend? You weren't born this way. No one is born this way. You were infected. It's a disease." Abraham squared his shoulders, as if he were expecting Dad to throw him a punch. "One that needs to be wiped out indefinitely."

Dad locked eyes with Abraham then and held his gaze for what seemed like an eternity. Viktor wondered if the look were a warning of some kind, or if the two of them were engaged in a silent conversation. Whatever it was, Viktor could tell that the fragile shell that had prevented them from being at one another's throats was cracking.

At long last, Dad tore his gaze away and turned back to his son. "Viktor . . . I have something to tell you. Don't be afraid. Everything is okay. But you need to know that I'm . . ."

The look in his dad's eyes as his words trailed off was beginning to frighten Viktor. His dad looked scared, and his dad had never looked that way before that Viktor could recall. "You're what, Dad?"

The air in the foyer felt heavy. It pushed down on Viktor's body until his shoulders ached. The silence between his words and those of his dad seemed to stretch on forever—a vast crevice of questions. His heart thumped hard against his ribs, drawing out a heavy bass line that filled his ears with its incessant pounding.

Dad released a crestfallen sigh. "Viktor, I'm . . . a vampire."

"And the truth shall set you free!" Abraham paused

between each word with nonverbal punctuation.

Viktor's heart beat once. Twice. Three times. Slow. Hard. Heavy inside of him. Was it some kinda sick joke? Another lie?

"What? A vam . . . but you're not a . . . they don't exist." His stomach clenched as he struggled to find meaning in his dad's words. He couldn't help but think that he and Damon may have discovered the truth if they'd just pushed Operation: Loch Ness a bit further and not given up so easily.

He wondered how many people his dad had killed. He wondered if his mom had any idea. He shook his head, frightened at the very idea that he might have been living his entire life sharing a home with a monster. "You can't be."

Abraham seemed almost celebratory in tone. "Oh, but I'm afraid he can be, Viktor, and he is. And not just any vampire—quite a famous one. Perhaps the most famous. Though not the oldest by far."

Somewhat subdued, Dad said, "Abraham, please. Let me. You owe me that much, at least."

But Viktor didn't want his father to intervene. He wanted to know everything that Abraham had to say on the matter. Everything that he'd ever not been told or had been lied to about. He needed answers. He deserved them. "What are you talking about?"

Abraham glanced at Viktor's dad, and something that Viktor couldn't identify passed between them. After a moment, Abraham said, "Your father is the one and only Dracula."

Viktor's heart pounded in his ears, blocking out all sound for a moment. "Dracula? Like the book? The one I'm reading in English?"

Abraham smiled, triumphant. "Yes. The real deal. Live and in person, for lack of a better word."

Viktor felt dizzy. His dad was a vampire. More than that, he was the most famous vampire. Dracula. *The* Dracula. As in, Bram Stoker, Nosferatu, Bela Lugosi, I-vant-to-suck-your-blood Dracula.

His dad dropped his eyes to the floor in shame—shame that Viktor wasn't 100 percent certain was deserved. Guilt filled his eyes as he looked at his son. "I'm sorry, Viktor. From the bottom of my heart. I should have told you years ago."

It was true. It was all true. His father was a vampire. An actual, real-life, bloodsucking, human-killing monster. His stomach twisted and turned. "I . . . does Mom know?"

"Yes. She knows. She's . . ." Dad trailed off, as if questioning how much he should share with his son.

Viktor set his jaw. What else didn't he know about his own family? "She's what?"

Abraham stood there, watching the uncomfortable exchange between father and son. He'd kicked over a hornet's nest and was now enjoying the carnage before him. Viktor had no idea what his dad had done to earn Abraham's venom, but Abraham seemed to revel in the moment and in Dad's pain.

And his dad *was* in pain—Viktor could see that much when he met his eyes. "She's a vampire as well, Viktor."

"What?" he choked. "Mom's a vampire too? How . . . why wouldn't you tell me? My whole life is a lie!"

His dad's voice cracked. "I'm sorry. Please forgive me. Forgive us."

"His mother's a vampire?" Abraham clucked his tongue. "Don't be so modest, Drake. She's not just another vampire. She's almost as famous as you are."

Viktor's head was spinning. He managed to calm the chaos inside his mind long enough to search his memory for another vampire almost as well known as Dracula but came up empty.

With a haughty demeanor, Abraham said, "Who knew the great Dracula and the notorious Elizabeth Bathory would ever fall in love, leave behind their notoriety, and move to the suburbs? No one, I assure you. It's a rather disappointing ending to your tale, my friend."

Elizabeth Bathory. Viktor knew that name. One of the books Mrs. Conrad had given him had talked about her a lot. She was that countess back in sixteenth-century Hungary who used to kill her handmaidens so she could bathe in their blood. The one who thought that by doing so, she could stay young forever.

Ruthven's words echoed in Viktor's mind. "*If the countess*

doesn't know about whatever it is that you have planned, it must be serious."

The countess. Mom. She was Elizabeth Bathory. His parents were actual, literal vampires. His mom and dad were infamous, supernatural creatures. And he . . . what would that make him?

CHAPTER TWENTY
The True Test of Friendship

Abraham reached behind him and when his hand reappeared, it was clutching something that gave Viktor pause. The obvious weapon in his hand was a wooden stake, tipped in silver. The time for conversation, it seemed, was over.

"Hold on," Viktor said. "Before anybody gets stabby or bitey, can we please just talk about this?"

His dad and Abraham glanced his way but returned to their conversation as if Viktor hadn't even spoken.

"I don't want to fight you, Abraham."

Abraham thrust his chin toward Viktor. "Then why did you bring backup?"

"I didn't. Viktor has nothing to do with this. I brought him here to meet you." Dad shook his head. There was a sadness in his tone, which was mirrored in his eyes. It seemed like hurting Abraham was the last thing in the world that he wanted to do.

Viktor thought back to his dad's conversation with Ruthven.

"Are you certain you won't change your mind about having him killed?"

"Certain enough. I'll mourn him, but what other choice do I have?"

His dad had been talking about Abraham the entire time. Not Viktor. Because his dad would never hurt him.

A guilty lump formed in Viktor's throat. How could he ever think that his dad could be so terrible? That his dad would ever plan to take his son's life? His dad was a monster, but he wasn't . . . well . . . a monster.

"You brought him here to meet me so that he'd know who to exact his revenge on, I suppose." Abraham was flipping the stake in his hand with expert skill, eyeing his friend with a look that said he was debating just how long to permit this conversation to continue.

"I brought him here . . ." Dad took a breath, as if preparing himself for another heated exchange. "So that he could see the face of my oldest friend and learn my deepest truth—the one thing strong enough to shatter our friendship into pieces."

Abraham snorted. "A truth I had to force you to reveal? If that were your intention, you wouldn't have required threats and prodding."

Dad nodded. "Perhaps I knew on some level that I needed your firm hand to ensure I'd share that truth with him, my friend."

Abraham stopped flipping the stake. Viktor had his eyes locked on the weapon, unable to tear his attention away. "We haven't been friends in a long time, Drake."

"Aren't we friends even now? Even after everything that's transpired between us?" His dad looked at Abraham. A long silence passed between them—one that spoke volumes. "You referred to me as *old friend* just moments ago. And even though I'm angry with you—so very angry for so long that I've almost forgotten what it's like not to feel so—I'm willing to admit that you are still my friend. My oldest and dearest friend. And I will lay aside everything ill-willed that's transpired between us over the years for the sake of preserving that friendship."

In response and without a moment's hesitation, Abraham tightened his grip on the stake in his hand and shook his head, his eyes locked on Viktor's dad like a predator to his prey.

With a sigh, Dad said, "So be it. I will give you what you want at long last, Abraham. I will fight you to the death. But first let Viktor go."

Viktor took a bold step between the two men and looked his dad in the eye. There was no way he was walking out of this room alone. He had to reason with his dad before somebody got killed. "I'm not going anywhere."

Both men chimed in unison, "Viktor—"

Viktor locked eyes with his dad. "Let's go home, Dad. We can talk about the vampire thing. Or not, if you don't want to. Can't we just go? Please."

After a long silence, in which it was pretty clear that his dad was weighing his options, he nodded, relenting. They were going home. And with any luck, Abraham was going to let them.

Quick movement to their left grabbed Viktor's attention as they turned to the door. At first, he thought that it was Abraham who was lunging at his dad, but when he whipped his head around, he saw someone completely unexpected. They were holding a stake and wearing a wild look in their eyes.

His heart aching, Viktor gasped. "Alys?"

The motion brushed her red hair back from her face, revealing her piercing emerald eyes, which were locked on Viktor's dad in fury. The way she moved told Viktor she wasn't new to this type of encounter, and that his dad wasn't the first she'd attacked. He wondered if she'd ever killed anyone before. He wondered if maybe she'd try to kill him too.

His dad pressed his attacker hard against the wall, knocking her stake onto the floor below and holding her there. A whiff of garlic was in the air. Viktor wondered if the weapon had been coated in it somehow.

Rather than look defeated, Alys just looked enraged. She fought against his dad, but he was too strong for her to wriggle free. Dad locked eyes with Abraham, who, much to Viktor's surprise, hadn't made the slightest move to protect his daughter. With a low growl, his dad said, "A shame you're raising your child to be a murderer."

The corner of Abraham's mouth twitched. "A hero, you mean."

Viktor's dad pressed his lips into a tight, thin line before parting them to speak. "So be it. Let's end this. Just you and me and the fragile thing I'd considered for so long to be our friendship."

"It will be my pleasure." Abraham flipped the stake over once more in his hand and readied the weapon, his eyes flashing with ages-old rage. "Old friend."

Dad barked, "Go home, Viktor. Now."

But Viktor wasn't going anywhere.

As Abraham lunged toward Viktor's dad, Viktor's dad closed his hand over Alys's shoulder and shoved her to the side—both, Viktor suspected, to distract his attacker and to get Alys out of the way so she didn't get hurt. Regardless of his reasons, Alys flew several feet before falling hard on her side. As soon as she hit the floor, she scrambled toward Viktor.

No, Viktor had time enough to think. *Toward something near me.*

He looked down just as her hand reached the wooden stake that she'd been holding before. Her fingers had just brushed against the wood when Viktor stomped his foot down on the weapon hard, pinning it in place. "What's wrong with you, Alys?! I thought we were friends!"

"Friends?" Alys scoffed as she brought herself to standing. "I told you, Viktor. I have a job to do, and that job is following my dad's orders."

Viktor's chest felt tight. "Didn't you say that sometimes you feel more like his employee than his daughter, and it's a job that you can never quit? Maybe you can't quit being his daughter, Alys, but that doesn't mean you have to do his blood-soaked bidding without question."

A glint of doubt and shame flashed in her eyes. "He's my dad, Viktor."

"But your dad's a killer." Viktor waved his arms at the situation unfolding around them. Dad and Abraham were struggling over control of the weapon in Abraham's hand. By the look of him, Viktor gauged that something was off about his dad. He seemed weaker, paler, as if he were sick. A worrisome feeling crept over Viktor, but he shook it off and drew his attention back to Alys. "This goes a little bit beyond a contest of 'my dad can beat up your dad' between friends, don't ya think?"

Alys's eyes narrowed. "But we're not friends, are we, Viktor?"

"What do you mean?" His brow fell into a crease that was a fraction of how deep his heart fell into his stomach. "Of course we are."

"Everything between you and me? It was all research. The

chats about books, the questions about what your parents do for a living, hanging out and sharing our feelings—all of it. Everything I did, I did for a reason."

It felt as if a large rock had been dropped into the bottom of Viktor's stomach from a high place. He couldn't believe it. He didn't want to believe it. "What about holding hands? Was that research too? What was the reason for that?"

Everything about her said that she was playing it cool. But her eyes betrayed a small glint of sorrow. Something that Viktor was both sad and elated to see. Setting her jaw, she said, "You can't possibly understand."

His attention was split so many ways, it was dizzying. Alys, his dad, Abraham, the stake beneath his foot. The last thing he needed added to the pile was heartbreak. "So, help me understand."

She shrugged, as if it would be obvious to anyone with half a brain—which kind of suggested that maybe she didn't think Viktor had half a brain. "My father and I needed intel. Our so-called friendship? That's all it was."

"That's a lie. The night I came over to watch a movie, you opened up to me. You said that you were scared. I saw it in your eyes that you meant it. Maybe more than anything. You couldn't have faked that." He swallowed hard, forcing the lump that had formed in his throat back down again.

She set her jaw, straightening some with confidence that Viktor wasn't convinced was authentic. "A Slayer is never scared."

"You were that night." He shook his head, the weapon beneath his foot never far from the surface of his thoughts.

There was movement to Viktor's right, drawing his attention. He glanced to see his dad crushing Abraham's stake to splinters with his bare hands. In response, with fury in his eyes, Abraham bodychecked Viktor's dad, slamming him against the door. When he hit the wood, he let out a groan.

It was just a glance, demanding maybe a few seconds at most, but it was long enough for Alys to take advantage and attack. Alys gripped Viktor's shoulder and kicked him hard in the back of his knee, knocking him forward. Sharp, hot pain shot through his leg. He'd pulled a muscle—he was almost certain—and it hurt more than anything he'd experienced to date. Viktor yelped before moving his foot back to stomp the stake in place, but it was too late. Alys was holding it in her hand, eyeing him with a fiery gaze that said that he wasn't walking out of this house without being more than a little familiar with pain. "Leave it alone, Viktor. Walk away now. Let me and my dad handle this situation, or I promise you, you'll limp for a week."

Joke's on you, Viktor thought as his knee throbbed in time with his heartbeat. *I'm already going to limp for a week. At least.*

He didn't have to consider his options. As far as he was concerned, there was only one. Viktor squared his shoulders and set his jaw. "I won't let you hurt him, Alys. Vampire or not, he's still my dad."

He didn't want to hurt his friend. He just wanted to stop her before she did something to break their friendship beyond repair; to protect his dad and go home again, leaving this all behind. Well . . . what he really wanted was to turn the clocks back, travel to the past, and never experience this moment at all, but that wasn't going to happen.

The loud crash of Abraham landing on the foyer table, smashing it to pieces, drew Viktor's and Alys's attention. As Abraham struggled to catch his breath, Viktor's dad paused, his eyes locked on the ring on Abraham's left hand. When he lifted his gaze to Abraham, the fury in his eyes was replaced by remorse.

Viktor didn't know what his dad had to feel guilty about, but whatever it was, it had something to do with Abraham's wife—that much was clear.

The sight of the remorse in Dad's eyes seemed to push Abraham over the edge. He jumped to his feet with a roar and lunged forward, shoving Viktor's dad backward into one of the pillars. Dad's head bounced off the marble and he crumpled to the floor, unconscious.

Abraham's chest rose and fell in pants. He stepped away from Viktor's unconscious father, eyeing the stake in Alys's hand. He wanted it—that much Viktor knew. He also knew that if Abraham got it, his dad was as good as dead.

With panting breath, Abraham said, "The world is far larger, far more dangerous than you realize, Viktor."

Glancing at Alys, Viktor said, "I can see that."

Alys remained still, as if she were well trained to pause her actions once her father became involved in a situation. She didn't look at Viktor. Rather, her eyes were focused on Abraham, as if awaiting further instructions from him.

"Viktor, my family tree lists a long line of Slayers, extending back to the very first vampire Slayer, my great-great-great-grandfather, Ernst Blomberg. One might say it's the 'family business.' More than that, it's the most important cause that any one person can undertake, let alone generations."

Viktor's jaw was so tight, it was beginning to ache. "If you're trying to impress me, you're wasting your time. I don't celebrate killers."

Alys parted her lips to speak, but Abraham silenced her with a look.

"We're proud of our history. But it's not like we can just hang out a sign, is it? 'Van Helsing and Sons.' Or should I say 'and Daughter'?" Abraham placed a hand on Alys's shoulder, and she smiled up at him with an expression that seemed only half sincere. Viktor could see that familiar glint of sadness within her gaze and felt sorry for her. It had to be so hard to have a father who'd push you to perform tasks that might go against every moral fiber of your being. But then . . . Viktor didn't know what was lurking inside Alys's mind. Maybe she'd been telling the truth about her loyalty to her father's cause. Maybe it was her cause too. Abraham continued, "Of course, my great-grandmother Elise was forced to change our last name centuries ago. Fame, after all, has its price."

Pulling himself away from his thoughts on Alys, Viktor raised his eyebrows. "Wait. Van Helsing? The vampire hunter? From Bram Stoker's *Dracula*?"

"That's the one." He took a slow step toward Alys, his eyes flicking from Viktor to the stake in her hands and back again.

Viktor took a step between the two. He wasn't sure why Abraham seemed so hesitant to just knock him to the side and grab the weapon, but he was grateful for it. "But if you're the real Abraham Van Helsing, how are you even alive still? Wouldn't you be like over a hundred years old?"

"As you must know based on our previous conversation, your father and I are very well acquainted." Abraham looked down at Dad's unconscious body then, a strange fog wafting over his expression. "After learning your father's secret, that he'd become a foul, bloodthirsty beast, I tried to end his life to no avail. Over the next few years, I tracked him, hunted him, battled him. At one point I realized that he wasn't aging, and that I was. If I wanted justice, I had to find a way to live for a period of time extending far beyond that of a typical human. I spent several years hunting down a little-known blood ritual."

This is my life now, Viktor thought. *A world where vampires are real, and their best friends take part in blood rituals so they can live long enough to kill them.* He had to try very hard not to roll his eyes at the absurdity of it all.

"It took a lot of hard work . . . and a lot of sacrifice in order to accomplish the task, but in the end, to my surprise and delight, it worked. I acquired what amounts to immortality." For a moment, Abraham seemed lost in thought, the wooden stake far from his mind, but soon the words came, bringing him back to the moment at hand and the weapon enclosed in Alys's fist. "So they say, anyway. The ritual made me as long-lived as a vampire, but without tainting my soul with vampiric traits. Unlike vampires, I do not require the consumption of human blood to go on surviving. But I also didn't acquire any of their skills, such as super speed or animorphing."

Animorphing? Viktor thought. But then he remembered the book *Dracula*, and how Dracula could morph into a wolf. The notion that vampires could maybe actually do such a thing was mind-boggling. What else were they capable of? What was *his dad* capable of?

Abraham continued, "Once it was done, I vowed to spend every minute of my life hunting your father. And now, it seems, that hunt is moments from coming to an end."

Viktor looked at Alys but kept an eye on Abraham with his peripheral vision. "Awful hypocritical of you to call my dad a killer when your family is full of killers, isn't it?"

For this, Alys had no response.

Viktor said, "Are you long-lived too, like your dad?"

Alys shook her head. "No reason for me to be—it's not

my fight. Dad's the only long-lived Slayer. That and his skills are why he's in charge of the Slayers."

"V-Viktor?" Dad sat up, touching his palm to the side of his head, where he'd hit the wall. He was dazed, bruised, and bleeding a little, but, to Viktor's great relief, otherwise unharmed.

"Dad! Are you okay?"

"I will be. I heal quickly." Viktor helped his dad stand. After he was vertical once again, his gaze found the window and a flash of fear entered his eyes. With a sense of urgency, he said, "This fight can wait. We have to get out of here."

With a hard look at the stake, Abraham moved in front of the door and barked, "I'm not letting you walk out this door alive, Drake."

Viktor considered asking what other way his dad could walk out the door but thought better of it.

Dad snapped his eyes to his friend. "I meant *all* of us. *We* have to get out of here. Someone is coming. By the look of that sky, she's almost here."

Abraham looked more than a little confused. The stake, it seemed, had been all but forgotten. For the moment, any-way. "Who's coming? What are you talking about?"

"Is it Lilith? How can you tell?" Viktor peered out the window. The sky was covered with dark, ominous clouds, and the wind had picked up, but otherwise his block looked just like it always did. "I don't see anybody out there."

"Lilith?" Abraham's eyes went wide. "What are you

talking about? Drake . . . what did you do?"

Dad sighed and looked up, as if the answer he was searching for might be on the ceiling. Apparently finding nothing up there, he looked at Abraham and confessed. "I summoned her."

"Are you insane?!" Abraham's voice bounced off the walls of the foyer in echoes. He sounded angry. But more than anything, he sounded afraid. "Why would you call forth the most wretched thing to ever walk the Earth?"

"I was angry and afraid for my family, Abraham. For my children." Dad's words came out sounding very much like an apology, but Viktor wasn't sure what his dad thought he should be sorry for.

A look of horror crossed Abraham's face, shadowed by shame. After a long pause, his shoulders sank, and he spoke with a soft tone. "I would never have harmed your children, Drake. I'm no monster."

It was Dad's turn to pause. "Neither am I."

He was looking at his old friend, trying hard to drive the point home. Viktor watched the scene with great curiosity, wondering if the reason his dad had never told him he was a vampire was because he didn't want Viktor to think of him as a monster either.

Alys tilted her head to the side, her eyes filled with questions. "Who's Lilith?"

Abraham looked at his daughter with fear lurking in his gaze. If he was trying to hide that fear, he wasn't doing a very good job of it. "Lilith is the mother of vampirekind. She's feared by everyone—vampire and Slayer alike. And for good reason."

Looking back and forth between her father and Viktor's dad, she said, "And that reason would be . . . ?"

After exchanging glances with Viktor's dad, Abraham turned back to his daughter and said, "Lilith has very unique abilities. She's powerful. Dangerous."

"No other vampire I've ever encountered can do what Lilith can do." Dad's voice was quiet. Something about his tone sent a chill up Viktor's spine.

Viktor said, "What's so special about her?"

"She can control the minds of anyone—human and vampire alike—and . . . worse things. Far worse." Dad shook his head, looking very much like he was reliving a memory.

Viktor furrowed his brow. "What could be worse than getting drained dry like a human Capri Sun?"

"The people she chooses not to devour"—Abraham swallowed hard, causing his Adam's apple to bob. It was hard to believe the four of them had been fighting just moments ago but were now united by what sounded like a common enemy—"become her victims in another, more savage way."

Dad spoke in a matter-of-fact tone. "Those whom she chooses become her spellbound loyal followers for the rest of their days—not that they have many days to live once in her grasp. During that time, she drains them of their life force until there's nothing left of the person they were at all."

Viktor's throat went dry. It was becoming hard to swallow.

Abraham shook his head in disbelief. "I can't believe you summoned Lilith, of all creatures, Drake."

"I made a mistake. I chose poorly." Dad's eyes fell to the ring on Abraham's left hand before rising again to meet Abraham's eyes. "As I have in many ways in the past."

"Why her? Why Lilith?"

Dad's voice came out sounding gruff, as if he were holding back tears that Viktor could not see. "Because I was afraid that I might have to kill you and I wasn't sure I could live with myself if I did that. I knew she would be up for the task . . . and that it would go quickly for you."

For a moment, Abraham said nothing. He and his old friend looked at one another. Abraham's voice was quiet when at last he broke the silence and said, "I'm grateful you warned me, so I won't take your life today. But you and I both know that day will come."

"I know a day will come when you'll try." Dismissing the warning as if he weren't worried about it at all, or he'd heard it a million times before, Dad looked down the hall. "I don't suppose this house has a safe room. It wouldn't stop her, but it might slow her down."

Outside the sky darkened more, in a way that could only be described as unnatural. Clouds swirled together, darkening from cotton white to asphalt black. No birds or squirrels were anywhere to be found. The temperature dropped sharply—from balmy summer warm to teeth-chattering winter chill. A strange electricity had filled the air, and the tiny hairs on the back of Viktor's neck stood on end. It felt like a storm was coming. But this was no ordinary storm. Once it arrived, life as they knew it would be over.

Dad snapped his eyes to Abraham. "How much garlic do you have in the house?"

Abraham shook his head. For the moment, their deadly rivalry had been forgotten. "None. The garlic juice I soaked my stake in was the last of it."

Viktor thought, *No wonder Dad seems weaker, even sick. I did smell garlic earlier. And it turns out vampires really are allergic to garlic after all.*

Dad cursed under his breath in frustration.

Alys chimed in, "Dad . . . I . . . are we really working with them? You said we had a job to do and would stop at nothing to do it."

"We can't very well do a job if we're dead. For now, count Drake and Viktor as momentary allies. Lilith must be our focus." Abraham's tone was one a boss might use with an employee. Viktor's heart sank for her. What she'd said about her relationship with her dad seemed 100 percent true.

"Now that I think about it, we may have some garlic salt, but . . . can you handle more exposure to garlic? You're weak enough as it is. How will you fight?"

Viktor's dad nodded. "I'll manage."

Alys disappeared into the kitchen and when she returned,

she handed a small bottle of garlic salt to Viktor's dad, who turned to face Viktor. "Viktor, take Alys into the basement and lock the door. Pour this in a line at the base of the door and in any windowsills you see. No matter what happens, you stay there and stay quiet. You hear me?"

As Viktor took the bottle in his shaking hand, he said, "What about you?"

At this, Drake and Abraham exchanged silent glances—an act that sent a shard of terror straight through Viktor's heart.

Alys's eyes were wide as they flicked around the room before settling on her father. "Dad?"

Abraham's voice warmed then toward his daughter—something Viktor thought was unusual for him. "It's okay, Alys. Go. Do as he says."

It took Alys a moment, but at last she nodded and led Viktor down the hall and into the basement. Viktor paused for a moment before closing the door and locking it. With trembling fingers, he sprinkled a thick line of garlic salt along the base of the door. By the time he reached the bottom of the stairs, Alys was pacing, looking very much like she didn't know what to do. Viktor found two windows, poured garlic salt where Dad had instructed, and turned to face her. "Are you okay?"

"Do I look okay?" The crease on her brow and the way she kept balling up her fists and fidgeting said that she was anything but, but Viktor didn't put voice to his thoughts.

She said, "I'm fine. I just wish my dad would let me help. I'm fully capable of killing a vampire."

Viktor bit his lip in contemplation before asking, "How many?"

"How many what?"

"How many have you killed?" It was such a strange thing that the last time he'd seen her they'd been discussing innocuous things, and now the topic was so very different. He wondered if they'd ever share a moment of normalcy again.

She hesitated before responding, as if she were embarrassed, but her expression didn't share that same sentiment. She looked angry. She looked sad. "None yet, but I will kill one. Probably soon."

His dad had referred to Alys as a murderer, which Viktor thought would be true of anyone who took another person's life. He didn't feel like Alys could kill someone. But then . . . he'd been wrong before. "You'd kill a person? Because, what, your dad told you to?"

Alys winced. "Viktor, I don't know how to break it to you, but your dad's not a person. He's a monster."

Viktor felt his muscles tighten in anger. There were a lot of things someone could say to him that he'd let go of, but attacking his family was off the table. "You have no idea what you're talking about."

Rolling her eyes, Alys said, "Please. You just learned that vampires exist, let alone the fact that your dad's one of them. You don't know your dad. Trust me. He's a monster."

All of a sudden, what sounded like the force of a tornado roared above them and both Viktor and Alys shot their attention to the ceiling.

"My dad's not a monster," Viktor said, his voice shaking. "But something tells me that Lilith is."

Screams echoed through the floor and into the basement, and just as Viktor was about to suggest that they hide, the basement door was ripped from its hinges and a horrible sound—one so terrifying that it made Viktor's teeth chatter—filled the air. Wood shattering into splinters, a grumble of something thunder-like. The smell of garlic filled the air as the garlic salt was blown away, the line that Viktor had poured at the bottom of the door broken. What followed was a woman's voice. Each syllable that she spoke was echoed by a child's mimicking whispers. "Come with me, children. I'm your mother now."

Viktor felt something stir within him. He set his jaw and said, "Alys . . . get behind me. We're not going anywhere."

CHAPTER TWENTY-ONE
Lilith Descends

Alys seemed to be frozen to the floor. Her wide eyes were locked on the basement stairs. Viktor imagined that she'd witnessed some scary stuff growing up with a Slayer for a father, so the fact that she looked terrified sent a worried whisper through his mind. He wasn't about to let some crazy vampire hurt her but wasn't certain how to stop it from happening. As quick as he could, he ran down a list in his mind of things he'd heard would hurt a vampire. Between *All the Vampires Everywhere* and the books Mrs. Conrad had given him, he thought he had a pretty good, albeit fictional, idea of what could work.

Silver was one option. Holy water, fire . . . what else? In the book, Dracula was taken down by knives. Was there anything stabby lying around?

He flicked his attention around the basement but didn't

see anything that would help him. Just furniture covered by sheets, an old trunk, several boxes, and a big plastic bin at the bottom of the stairs containing a variety of items—an old cane, some gardening tools, a few umbrellas, and an old baseball bat. It was said that sunshine could kill them, but Lilith had brought her own storm. Plus, his dad loved a sunny day, so Viktor didn't think that some time in the sun would do much of anything, apart from put her at risk for skin cancer. There was beheading, but that was out of the question as well, unless he could find something sharper than the baseball bat. Viktor straightened with hope as the last item on his list flitted through his mind. He bent down and plucked a chunk of the broken door from the floor. A wooden stake. Sure, it wasn't hand-carved or blessed by some priest or anything—not that he had any idea if those things were a requirement—but it was wooden, and it was sharp. He stepped in front of Alys, who was still frozen to the spot, and widened his stance, his fingers whitening as they curled around his makeshift stake.

Just as abruptly as the terrifying sounds had begun, they ceased, leaving the basement in a silence so empty that it raised goose bumps all over Viktor's arms. Had his dad or Abraham taken out Lilith at the last minute?

There was the small squeak of wood as someone began their descent down the basement stairs. Viktor held his breath, hoping he'd see his dad's sneakers or even Abraham's tasteful leather loafers.

Instead, he saw the bare feet of a pale, petite woman as

she glided down the stairs, hands at her side. She was dressed in a simple gown—silk, white, and wispy. Around her neck was a necklace that looked like it was made of silver, but must have been white gold or platinum, because it wasn't hurting her at all to wear it. Her hair was raven black, her eyes bright turquoise. She didn't look like some super-old bloodthirsty monster. She looked like a young woman in her twenties. One who wrote poetry about love and loss, who insisted on going barefoot so she could connect with the earth on a spiritual level and ate a vegetarian diet. But he knew that she was anything but those things. She was a vampire. From what his dad had said, she was *the* vampire.

As she reached the bottom of the stairs, Viktor tightened his grip on his stake and said, "Stay back."

His voice shook more than he'd intended.

A soft smile danced on Lilith's pink lips. The look in her eyes was one of familiarity, though Viktor couldn't even hazard a guess why. "Hello, Viktor. It's good to see you. You've grown into such a strong young man."

Shc knew his name. And it sounded like she might know even more about him. His chest tightened; his stomach clenched. The fear and confusion that he had been feeling swelled into a full-blown panic attack. He hadn't even known that vampires were something that existed. And now the most powerful vampire in the world was talking to him like they were old acquaintances who hadn't seen one another in a very long time. He swallowed hard and did all that he could to feign confidence. "You aren't hurting anyone."

"You're right." The corner of her mouth tugged upward in a small smile. "Unless you make me."

It was a threat, but maybe a warning as well, and Viktor had zero idea how he was going to stop her if she made a move against them. Beside him, Alys remained silent.

Lilith's voice came out sounding almost like a purr. "I just wanted to extend an invitation to you both to join me. What do you think? Would you like to join me in a new life—one with magic, unfailing love, and our forever family?"

Viktor scoffed. How dumb did she think they were? "Of course we don—"

"Yes. I want that. More than anything," Alys said, her tone soft, even anxious.

Viktor's eyes shot to Alys in shock. She wore a dreamy, far-off look that chilled him to the bone. "Alys? What are you doing?"

Alys didn't meet his gaze. "I'm going to be with my family, Viktor. My sisters."

"I don't under—" Realization hit him hard. Lilith must be controlling her mind. Why wasn't Lilith controlling his? "She must be controlling you somehow. Remember what my dad said? She can control minds. What you're feeling and thinking aren't real!"

"My thoughts are real. I know what I'm doing." Alys stepped forward, almost floating. She looked like a person wading into warm, beautiful waters after a long walk through the desert.

He reached out to grab Alys by the shoulder, but Alys quickened her pace before he could and hurried to Lilith's side. Viktor shook his head. "This isn't you, Alys. It's Lilith. She's making you feel those things."

Lilith cupped Alys's chin with her palms for a moment, smiling into Alys's eager gaze. Alys looked at Viktor and said, "Come with us, Viktor. Come be a part of our family. Our fathers haven't been good to us. We deserve more. We deserve better."

Seeing Alys so easily manipulated both saddened him and frightened him. He wished he could say that it infuriated him, but anger was far from his mind, buried beneath miles of anguish and helplessness. "How do you know what she's offering us is better, Alys? She's putting that in your head. Don't believe her."

Lilith faced Viktor then, looking more than a little confident and triumphant. "She's right, you know. I can offer you peace and understanding. I'll love you and fulfill your every need, your heart's desire. Most importantly . . . I will always tell you the truth."

Alys beamed, and a wave of disgust passed over Viktor. What was he going to do?

A small line creased her forehead. Her lip twitched. Tilting her head to the side, she examined him for a moment, as if he were a new exhibit in a museum of curiosities. As if she couldn't quite put her finger on what was happening between them.

Then it hit Viktor. She couldn't control his mind. Why? What was so special about him and his dad that she couldn't do what seemed to come so easily to her? His dad was a vampire, but Viktor . . . Viktor wasn't anything special at all. He was just an average, ordinary twelve-year-old kid.

Apparently, one who couldn't be controlled by the most powerful vampire in existence.

A splinter of confidence straightened his shoulders. He still had no idea how he was going to stop her, stake or no stake, but at least he had his mind. "You can't control me. And you can't take my friend away from me. I won't let you."

Her expression said that she didn't care one bit about what he was saying or worry at all about whether he was right that he could thwart her plans to take Alys with her. But something dark lurked in her eyes—something that told Viktor that the wind raging outside wasn't the only storm. Inside Lilith, something far more dangerous was brewing. He guessed she didn't get told no a lot.

She pursed her lips before closing her eyes for a moment, as if gathering her sense of calm. When she opened her eyes, she looked to be in control once more, but Viktor could see that the storm inside her was still brewing. "It's your decision to join me or not, Viktor, just as it's Alys's. She's made her decision. So now that that's settled, you and I can get on with the unfinished business between us."

He didn't want to engage in any more conversation than was necessary, but the curiosity she'd piqued was impossible for him to resist. "What business? What are you talking about?"

"I'm talking about the thing in your hand and the fact that you are holding it, with the intent of harming me." Her tone sounded kind enough, but he could detect the hint of anger beneath her words as she spoke. "I'm afraid I must insist that you drop that sad excuse for a weapon. You want to, don't you? Let it go, Viktor. I can give you anything you wish. Unbreakable friendship, loyalty, anything at all. But first, you need to put the wooden shard away."

He tightened his grip on the makeshift weapon, knowing that she was trying to gain control of his mind. Trying . . . and failing. "No way. Now let Alys go."

Surprise lit up her face, with a side of confusion. Tilting her head to the side, she lifted her falling smile and said, "You are a curious thing, Viktor. I should like to get to know you better. Don't you want to be my friend?"

"Not even a little, lady. Now get away from her and leave us alone or I'm putting this hunk of wood right through your chest. I've seen movies." He cringed at the last sentence. Right up until that, he thought he'd sounded like such a tough guy. *Way to screw it up at the end, Viktor,* he thought. *I'm sure she's totally intimidated by a dude who gets all his attack moves from Netflix.*

Lilith flicked her gaze to Alys, who was looking at her like she was the hero in Alys's favorite book, and then looked back at Viktor, her tone sharpening some. "I must insist you put the stake down, Viktor. Now."

Confidence filling him, he straightened and said, "Bite me, Lilith."

Lilith clenched her jaw, fire lighting up her turquoise eyes. Her fists were balled, her fingers paling from the pressure. He immediately regretted his choice of words and couldn't help but think that she looked a lot like Celeste did in the first grade when Tommy Alderson had refused to share the brownie he'd brought to school in his lunch box.

Through gritted teeth, Lilith growled. "So be it. I'm more than happy to oblige."

Lilith lunged forward so fast that Viktor almost didn't have time to register that she was moving. She hit him with such force that he flew backward into the support pole at the center of the room. His head hit the pole hard, flinging his body into a midair spin. A shock of stark white filled his field of vision before everything went dark. When he came to again, his vision returned to blurry, at best. He slumped forward, almost unable to move. He looked around and spotted what he believed to be a familiar shape on the ground across the room. The makeshift stake. He'd dropped it when Lilith hit him. He needed to grab it again.

Alys needed him to grab it again.

He could hear Lilith speaking, but the ringing in his ears

wouldn't allow him to understand what she was saying. His muscles screaming, Viktor remained face down and began inching his way across the floor toward what he believed to be the stake. If he could maintain the element of surprise, they just might have a chance to get out of this alive. Also, aside from his brilliant plan to imitate all his favorite action movie stars and video game heroes with the best stealth and surprise that he could muster, Viktor wasn't sure that he could have managed to stand up, even if he had wanted to. Was he feeling this way because she'd bounced his brain off a concrete pillar, or was it the added nuisance of some unidentified vampire skill she'd unleashed on him? He didn't know. He just knew that if he had to crawl to that stake, he was going to do it. No matter how much it hurt.

Struggling to find the energy, he pulled himself across the cool concrete floor toward the blur that he was pretty sure was the splintered hunk of wood that he'd dropped. He hoped Alys had her attention glued to the vampire in front of her, and not on him. He knew he looked ridiculous, not exactly like the conquering hero from the movies and games that he was trying to emulate.

As he made his way closer to the stake, and by default closer to Lilith and Alys, he heard something clear as a bell that sent his heart racing. Lilith said, "Come now, Alys. I'll introduce you to the rest of your new family, and together we'll dispatch that Slayer father of yours. As a treat, I'll even let you kill Drake yourself when we're done."

She spoke in the same way a parent might offer some ice cream to a child if they finished all their vegetables.

She hadn't sensed him getting closer to her. That, or she had, and dismissed him as not much of a threat at all. She also hadn't even tried to bite him, which made him wonder why. Had whatever it was that made him uncontrollable also made him unpalatable?

With dismay, Viktor realized that the stake was farther away than he'd thought. Lilith clearly believed him to be out of commission and no longer a threat—if she indeed had ever viewed him as such. As she grasped Alys's hand and turned toward the steps to leave, Viktor knew this was his last chance. If he didn't act now, another opportunity was not likely to present itself. There was no way he could reach the stake in time. Thinking quickly, he summoned all the strength he could and reached out, grabbing Lilith's ankle midstep. He yanked his hand back with all his might and, to his relieved surprise, the vampire fell forward. If he could knock her down, maybe he'd have time to get to the stake. And if he could do that, maybe he could summon the will and energy that he'd need to take her out of commission forever.

The moment her balance faltered, Viktor's brain must have sensed that all was not lost. They might have a chance of getting out of this alive. But, to do that, his brain would have to start working at full capacity again. Well, 80 percent capacity would do. His vision came back into sharp focus just in time for him to see Lilith's eyes widen in horrified realization as she landed hard against the boxes and plastic bins at the bottom of the stairs. Viktor heard Alys gasp but didn't realize right away what had happened. Then he saw it.

The plastic bin had been full of gardening tools. Lilith lay on the floor covered in rakes, shovels, and other lawn-care implements. Boxes covered her head, but beneath the pile of boxes, yard tools, and one very unpleasant vampire lady was an expanding pool of reddish-black liquid. Lilith had impaled herself on the handle of what looked to be an old cane. Blood covered the wood in a horrific, metallic-smelling dark burgundy paint job.

Viktor's stomach rolled. He knew he was going to be sick. He made his way to standing and did all that he could to keep his stomach contents on the inside. He'd never seen a dead body before, human or not. But he had to know for sure that it was all over. He had to be certain that Lilith was dead.

When the nausea had begun to subside, Viktor pushed himself to standing. With absolute caution he moved closer to the bin. That's when the pile began to move and moan. His eyes widened with horror as he saw the arm of what he had hoped was a corpse place its hand on the floor and push itself up to stand.

Lilith was still alive.

She blinked, her eyes finding Alys with a questioning look she didn't give voice to. She coughed then, sending a thick line of blood dribbling down her chin. When she met

Viktor's gaze, she chuckled, but it came out sounding more like a gurgle. "A lucky shot, boy. But I'm sure you're far more surprised by the outcome than I."

She came to standing, the cane protruding from the right side of her chest. "For future reference, you have to pierce my heart for a stake to work. And that would be over here."

As she spoke, Lilith was pulling the curved piece of wood from her chest. It made a seeping, suctioning sound as the fibers of the wood strained against the sinews of flesh. Once it was free of her chest, there was a wet, sucking sound. The cane may not have hit the heart, but it sounded like it had at least punctured a lung. Not that it mattered much; that was a wound that a vampire would easily heal from over time. Now that the piece was in her hand, Lilith used the blunt end of her would-be instrument of death to punctuate the final words of her sentence, thumping it against her chest over where her heart resided.

Her words spoken, and her point made that she was not out of this fight yet, Lilith hurled the bloodied cane to the floor and lunged for Viktor.

What she had not seen was what Alys had been doing this whole time. As her attention was focused on Viktor, Alys had been inching closer to where the discarded stake lay on the floor.

Just as Lilith lunged, Alys dropped, grabbing the stake and tossing it to Viktor. In one swift motion that would have made any of his imaginary heroes proud, Viktor caught the stake, spun out of the way of Lilith's lunge, and plunged the hunk of wood into her chest.

"Duly noted," he said.

The light began to fade from Lilith's eyes, but right before it did, she said, "You should know, Viktor . . . that your mother was part of my family . . . before your father killed her."

CHAPTER TWENTY-TWO
The Messy Details

Viktor steered Alys away from Lilith's corpse and up the stairs. By the time they reached the foyer, she'd ceased her frightened shivers, but she still looked pale from fear—and maybe something more. He had no idea what the effects of breaking her mind free from Lilith's grasp were. His stomach twisted into knots as it occurred to him that he was a murderer. He'd taken a person's life. A horrible vampire person, but a person still.

"Are you okay?"

Alys was so pale, it looked like she'd lost a lot of blood, but Viktor couldn't see any physical injuries at all. Her lips were trembling. "Is . . . is she dead?"

"I think so." He glanced back at the door to the basement. "I hope so."

Someone was pounding on the front door, but then, without anyone touching it, the door unlocked and opened, as if it had been held by some unseen force. Viktor thought about Lilith's abilities that he'd witnessed and wondered just how powerful she had been.

Dad and Abraham burst into the house, ready for a fight. When they saw their offspring, they exchanged confused glances. With a shaking voice, Viktor said, "Dad . . . I killed Lilith."

Hot tears welled in his eyes. They were left over from the trauma and stress of the experience, but he still felt stupid for crying in front of Alys, who was being hugged by her father. Viktor's dad said, "You . . . killed . . . Lilith?"

Viktor nodded, drying his eyes with the back of his hand.

Dad said, "Show me."

Viktor led his dad down the basement stairs. He prepared himself to see the dead creature again and told himself to keep it together and not vomit at the sight of her. But when he reached the bottom step, something far worse was awaiting them. An empty room.

Lilith's body was nowhere to be seen. Her blood wasn't on the cane's handle. The stake was gone. She and all evidence of her death were nowhere to be found. Viktor searched the basement, but there was nothing Lilith-related there. No proof that he'd just vanquished an evil, monstrous foe at all. Shaking his head, confounded, he said, "I don't get it. She was right here. She—"

"She's gone." Fear crossed his dad's eyes. "Viktor . . . Lilith is still alive. You're very fortunate to have frightened her away, but she's still alive somewhere, and someday, she will want retribution. Of that I have no doubt."

Viktor's stomach sank. On one hand, he was relieved he wasn't a murderer after all. But on a much more prevalent hand was the fact that he'd just managed to tick off the most dangerous vampire in the world.

"Don't tell your mother," Dad said, the fear in his eyes unrelenting. "I don't want her to worry."

Lilith's words echoed inside Viktor's mind. ". . . *your mother was part of my family . . . before your father killed her.*"

Viktor nodded, agreeing to something he'd yet to consider. But his thoughts weren't on his dad and his request for secrecy at all.

They were consumed by the empty basement, and Lilith . . . and where she might be now.

CHAPTER TWENTY-THREE
Mortal Cravings

No matter how hard she tried to stop, Alys was still trembling. The conversation between her father, Drake, and Viktor as they said their goodbyes was nothing more than a blur of sounds that she didn't recognize as words, really. She knew they were talking but couldn't sharpen her attention enough to identify who was speaking or what it was that they were saying. It felt like her head was full of a dense fog that refused to dissipate.

She squeezed her eyes shut and opened them again, focusing as much as she could. Standing in front of her was her father, his forehead creased in concern. Viktor and Drake had gone. It was time, she assumed, for her debriefing. "I've failed. Again. So, let's start with that."

Abraham held up a hand, shaking his head. "There will be time for a debriefing later. First tell me if you're okay."

Alys blinked in confusion. Was he actually asking about her well-being? There really was a first time for everything, she thought. "I . . . I'm fine."

"Did she hurt you?"

"No. She . . . she wanted me to join her. To become part of her family."

"Lilith is a very powerful creature, child. You're lucky she didn't kill you."

Lucky? It was an interesting choice of words, Alys thought. She didn't feel lucky. Rather, she felt like she'd just been united with the perfect mother figure, only to have her ripped away forever—leaving Alys with nothing but an aching hole at the center of her being that would never be filled. "Yeah. I suppose I am."

The look in his eyes wasn't one she'd ever witnessed before. He looked worried. About her. Abraham gave her shoulder a squeeze but said nothing. Instead, he moved past her and began picking up the shattered remains of the basement door.

Alys watched him in silence. If he had only hugged her and told her everything would be all right, she might have burst into tears and begun to heal from the trauma of the evening. But he hadn't. He'd done what any good Slayer would do. He got to work finishing the job.

And Alys was left with the not-difficult task of debating which family she would prefer to be a part of. The one she was born to . . . or the one she craved.

CHAPTER TWENTY-FOUR
The Truth of the Matter

The following morning, after the deepest sleep of his life, Viktor was walking down the stairs after the longest, hottest shower he'd ever had, when he heard his dad call from the living room. His stomach tensed with dread. He didn't want to relive the horrors of the night before. He didn't want to discuss his dad's vampiric nature. Truth be told, he just wanted to forget the whole thing and go back to life as usual.

"Viktor, come in here, please." Dad's voice was subdued, and when Viktor walked into the room, he could see his dad's face wore an expression to match. "Sit down, son. We need to talk."

Viktor crossed the room without saying a word.

His dad gauged him for a moment, then took a sip of his coffee and said, "What can I tell you? What do you want to know?"

"The truth. The entire truth. Anything. Everything. I mean, I'm still processing everything, but . . ."

His dad nodded. "Of course."

Viktor considered asking what Lilith had implied about his mother but thought better of it, chalking it up to Lilith's evil, manipulative ways. Mulling it over for a moment, Viktor settled on what should be an easy question for his dad to answer. "What happened to you and Abraham last night? Everything went quiet right before Lilith came downstairs, and you two were just . . . gone."

"Lilith cannot control my mind. But she can control Abraham's, which she did. He attacked me, forcing me outside, where we fought. Or rather, where he attacked me repeatedly and I thwarted his advances. Something must have muddied Lilith's focus, because at one point, her control over him relinquished completely. I suspect it was the cane through her chest." His dad looked amused at his quip, but his bemusement faded away the moment he saw the expression that Viktor was wearing. Viktor didn't find any aspect of their encounter with Lilith to be funny at all. "Realizing he was free at last, we tried the door and found it was held fast. We began pounding on it, hoping to force it open, but then it swung open, and we found you and Alys there, to our great relief, alive and unscathed."

Viktor nodded in understanding. "So . . . you and Mom are Dracula and Elizabeth."

"We are."

Viktor thought for a second before saying, "What about

Aunt Carmilla? She's your sister. Does she know you're a vampire?"

"She ought to." Dad paused then, as if maybe he was beginning to wonder how much he should tell his son. But it was too late. He'd told Viktor to ask him anything, that he would tell him the truth. "She's a vampire as well."

"Oh. I see . . ." His stomach tensed then. It felt like his whole world was on the verge of falling apart. He swallowed hard, trying to keep it together. "And Aunt Laura?"

"Yes. Her too."

His dad, his mom, his aunts. How many other vampires did he know? How many people in his life had been lying to him about who and what they were? "Tell me more about Lilith. Who is she?"

"Lilith is, as far as anyone knows, the very first vampire to ever exist. She's quite powerful, as you now know. What she did is barely scraping the surface of her abilities." Something crossed his eyes then—something resembling fear, but so much darker, somehow.

"So why call her for help with Abraham then? I mean, if she's so dangerous. Even for you. Seems like a crazy, stupid risk, Dad."

"Your mother would agree, and in hindsight, I do as well." Dad took a second to gather his thoughts, then said, "Lilith owes me a . . . considerable favor after I did one for her some years back. As you now understand, Abraham and I have a long, rather sordid history. We were best friends.

In many ways, we're still friends even now. But many years ago, he discovered my true nature after I hurt someone who he loved deeply—not on purpose, mind you—but Abraham has never been able to forgive me."

Dad's eyes reddened, as if tears were fighting their way to the surface no matter how hard he tried to keep them contained. "He's chased me for years, seeking revenge. And he's gotten close a few times. I'd hoped that we were free of his want of vengeance after moving to America. But I was foolish to think that was possible. I needed it to end, and I thought Lilith was the way to end it."

And here Viktor thought his friendship with Damon was complicated at times. He couldn't imagine having a best friend who wanted you dead. Like, in-the-ground, dirt-nap dead. "So the person Abraham loved . . ."

"Suffice it to say . . . he had a wife once. And I am the reason he doesn't anymore."

"What about that Ruthven guy? He talked about you like you're royalty or something."

"Ruthven is one of the few vampires I still feel that I can trust. He served under me on the Romanian council. I knew if I summoned him, he would come, he'd keep our meeting secret, and he'd do as I asked without any real argument."

"There was a word he used—one that's written in your copy of *Dracula*. Elysia. What does it mean? Is it a person? A place?"

"No, son. Elysia isn't a person or a place. It's more like

a concept. It's what vampires feel when they are together. Humans cannot understand it. Not really." His dad's attention drifted then, but only briefly, as if he were recalling some memory that troubled him. "I must say, I'd forgotten about the inscription."

Viktor thought about asking about the council his dad had mentioned but thought he should ask the question that was burning through his core. "Have you ever . . . killed anyone? Like humans? Like . . . for food?"

Dad winced, like he was hoping he'd never have to answer that question. "Yes. But I try not to kill humans anymore. Your mother and I subsist mostly on donated human blood."

Mostly. Viktor's stomach twisted into knots. "What about that woman I saw you chasing the other night?"

Dad sat there in silence for a long time, which was an answer of sorts on its own. When at last he spoke, it seemed like he'd chosen every word with immense care. "There is an issue that comes with drinking blood that's not taken directly from the vein. You see . . . drinking from the source enhances certain abilities as well as strength. Knowing that I would be facing Abraham, I needed to make certain that I was in top form for that encounter."

He'd killed her. His dad had murdered a woman in cold blood. Viktor felt sick. He felt angry. But mostly, he felt disappointed. "So . . . you . . ."

"No, son. I'd planned to, but in the end, I couldn't bring myself to harm another person like that. I was terrified that Abraham might hurt you, your sister, your mother, your aunts. I needed to be strong enough to protect you all. But I had to find another way." Both his dad's words and expression seemed sincere. "So, I broke into the butcher shop downtown and drank every drop of cow's blood that I could find, hoping it would be enough."

The nausea that had been rising in Viktor's throat subsided. His dad may be a vampire, but at least he wasn't a cold-blooded murderer.

Dad cleared his throat before saying, "Now, if you don't mind, son, I have a few questions of my own. The biggest of those questions being . . . Viktor, how are you still alive? You're human. Lilith should have been able to control your mind with little effort."

Viktor furrowed his brow. "But how am I human, Dad? You and Mom are vampires. Wouldn't that make me one too?"

Once again, Lilith's words clung to his mind like cobwebs. *". . . your mother was part of my family . . . before your father killed her."*

What did it mean? He was almost too afraid to ask.

"No. You are human, son."

"But . . . how do you know?"

Dad took in a deep breath and blew it out slow, as if settling his nerves some for the part of the conversation they were now entering. "Because your birth mother was human."

Birth mother? Viktor's heart all but stopped. But that would mean—

"It's complicated. How did it all get so complicated?" Dad stood up and began pacing back and forth across the room. "Your mother and I emigrated to North America long ago. There were certain . . ."

"Complications?" Viktor's head was still spinning. Were his parents not his parents? Had he been adopted by vampires? If there were a list of things that he thought he had to be concerned about, whether he'd been adopted by bloodthirsty monsters was nowhere near it.

"Yes. Complications. There were complications in the vampire world, a world we refer to as Elysia, that we had no choice but to flee. So, we ran, and we hid and created new lives for ourselves in the new world, though it wasn't all that new by the time we got here."

"What happened to my birth mother?"

"Right." A sharp slice of guilt crossed his gaze then. "I never knew her name. When I found her, I'd been subsisting on the blood of animals and donated human blood for a matter of decades. It was a difficult transition. Your mother handled it far better than I. I had gone for an evening stroll to clear my mind of the hunger. Your birth mother had just been the victim of an attack. I don't know if it was a mugging gone wrong or what have you, but she was lying there in the alley, bleeding to death."

The room seemed so quiet. The only sounds that reached Viktor's ears were his father's voice, shaking with what he presumed was guilt, and his own heartbeat, which was thumping along in a surprisingly calm manner. But then, once you've faced off against the most dangerous vampire to have ever existed, what else was there to get upset about?

"One moment she was lying there, her heart slowing. The next moment she was in my arms, and I was feeding on her. It happened so fast. I lost control. It was only afterward that I realized she was pregnant with you. So I delivered the baby as quickly as I could, wrapped you in a blanket, and whisked you off to your mother. I explained what happened and she never hesitated to embrace you as our son. Not for a moment." He snapped his gaze to Viktor's then. His eyes were shimmering with the threat of tears. "It is my greatest shame that I took that woman's life, Viktor, and the greatest gift that I have you as my son. I cannot express how terrible I feel."

Viktor dried his own tears with the back of his hand. "Would she have lived if you'd left her alone?"

"No. The stab wounds were too deep, too many." Dad sat beside Viktor on the couch then, his tone warm and caring. He was being the father that Viktor knew him to be, which was so confusing, it made Viktor dizzy. He said, "I won't ask you to forgive me, as I can never forgive myself. Your mother and I have made it our mission to protect you from all harm—and to honor the life that was lost that day. We love you, Viktor."

"What about Hannah? Is she—"

"Hannah is adopted. Vampires . . . we . . . we can't have children. Not in the way that humans do. Apart from an old wives' tale, that is." He shook his head, casting away whatever invasive thoughts had entered his mind. "Hannah. She's still your sister."

"I never said she wasn't." Genetics didn't matter to Viktor.

His family was his family, no matter what. Lilith's words floated through his mind. "*You should know, Viktor . . . that your mother was part of my family . . . before your father killed her.*" He swallowed hard and said, "To answer your question, Dad, I don't know how Lilith was unable to control me. She just . . . couldn't."

"Interesting." A silence fell between them then, but before Viktor could be the one to end it, his dad said, "I should call your mother and tell her to come home. I'm sure she and your aunts must be worried."

Viktor nodded and Dad went to pick up the phone and call Mom. After having received way more information than he had been prepared to know, Viktor sat there, absorbing everything that his dad had told him. It felt like his life had changed overnight, but the truth of it was, it hadn't really changed at all. It was just that he now understood that what he thought had been his life . . . *hadn't.* And he didn't quite know how to feel about it.

Two days later Viktor was sitting on his balcony with Damon, whose jaw was still on the floor after Viktor had caught him up on the details of the harrowing event. His left hand was bandaged where he'd apparently cut himself during the encounter with Lilith. His bruised body still ached. His head still felt weird and spacy at times. But he was alive. And his family was safe—as were Alys and her dad, as far as he knew.

Down below, Viktor's dad was walking across the street to Abraham, who was finishing up some trimming around his mailbox. The two chatted for a while like normal suburban neighbors—not at all like a vampire and his slayer.

Damon followed Viktor's gaze to where the men stood and said, "So they're still friends? After all of that?"

Viktor's neck hurt as he shook his head, tearing his attention away from the scene across the street. "I don't know. To be honest, I don't want to know. I don't care. I'm just glad they're both okay."

Damon gawked at him like he had seven heads or something. "How can you not want to know what's going on between them? After everything you saw. Everything you learned. Aren't you even a little curious if they're going to try to kill each other?"

"No, Damon." The truth was, he and his dad hadn't talked about any of it after that morning in the living room. He was willing to bet that Dad also wanted to just put it behind them. He didn't know how much Dad had told his mom or aunts, and he didn't ask. But he did think about Hannah, and the fact that she deserved to know the truth one day. Not now. But soon.

Damon glanced across the street once more before meeting Viktor's gaze again. Viktor could tell his best friend was doing all that he could to understand, but he wasn't able to do so just yet. "Why not?"

"I want to go back to life in the middle of Nowhere. I want

to pretend that none of it ever happened." He knew that he couldn't make Damon understand. But maybe Damon didn't need to understand. Maybe Damon just needed to respect that Viktor wanted to act like the whole thing had only been a bad dream.

Damon said, "Bro, you can pretend all you want. But you can't change the fact that your dad is Dracula, and your mom is Elizabeth Bathory. No amount of denial can take that away from reality."

He hadn't told Damon about his birth mother. It didn't feel right to share that with anyone. Not yet. Not until he'd had some time to process it all.

Viktor opened his mouth to respond, but then he noticed Alys standing in her window, watching him. He raised his hand and waved, wishing very much that things could be different between them—that they weren't both caught up in a situation that felt impossible, that they could go back to a simpler time when vampires weren't real, and her father wasn't a Slayer. But they were long past that now.

Without waving back, Alys closed her curtains.

A sinking sadness filled Viktor then, so he combated it by looking at the one positive thing he could think of that had come from this whole mess.

At least he'd gotten over his fear of talking to girls.

ACKNOWLEDGMENTS

There are a lot of people who've supported me throughout my return to Elysia, but the two that matter the absolute most are my children, Jacob and Alex. Jacob and Alex, you two have given me more support and more love than a single person ever deserves. You've respected (and protected) the bubble, acted as wonderful assistants whenever I've needed one (or, at times, two), and have never failed to believe in me and my abilities—even when I was struggling to do so for myself. You're terrific people, and truly, truly, the loves of my life. Thank you.

I would be remiss if I failed to thank the greatest literary agent that planet Earth has ever known, Michael Bourret of Dystel, Goderich & Bourret. Michael, you've been there through the highest peaks and deepest valleys of my career.

You've supported me at every turn, encouraged me when I desperately needed it, and have been an amazing friend every step of the way. The publishing world (and the world at large) is a better place for having you in it. Thank you for being you.

Endless appreciation and gratitude go to my editor, Karen Chaplin. Karen, you didn't even know the world of Elysia, but upon meeting Viktor, you let us take you by the hand and drag you into a world of weirdness that I call home—and you've yet to bat an eye. Thank you for teaching me how to be a better writer, and for helping me bring readers back to this world when they never thought they'd have the chance.

A mountain of gratitude goes to Rosemary Brosnan, who's championed me and my work for many years, and always offered a sympathetic ear and a helping hand. You're a good friend, Rosemary. Thank you. For everything.

Thank you to my wonderful team at HarperCollins, for putting your best foot forward and kicking absolute butt to support one of my favorite books to date. Without you—all of you—my Minion Horde would not be able to return to Elysia for fresh stories, new secrets, and all the heartbreak and bloodstains that come with it. Thank you for helping me bring *The Chronicles of Viktor Valentine* to life.

But I can't just thank my team at HarperCollins. I also need to thank my team over at Penguin Random House, because that's where this all began in the first place. Thank you—all of you—for helping me bring *The Chronicles of*

Vladimir Tod into the world. Without Vlad, Viktor simply would not be.

Many thanks to Matt Schu for creating the most beautiful Edward Gorey–esque cover I have ever seen. You're brilliant. Keep shining.

Last, but certainly never least, I want to thank my Minion Horde. So many of you have been with me for such a significant portion of your lives. You've shared with me, and I with you. We've all grown and changed and lived. But deep inside our hearts, we're all sitting at the Crypt, just waiting for any sign that Elysia has not left us. And I'm thrilled to report that no, Minions, Elysia never left you . . . and it never will. Thank you for following me—all the way from Bathory to Nowhere . . . and beyond.